Speaking to
№· 4

a novel

Speaking to No. 4

a novel

Alta Ifland

New Europe Books

Williamstown, Massachusetts

Published by New Europe Books, 2022
Williamstown, Massachusetts
www.NewEuropeBooks.com

ISBN: 978-1-7345379-7-0

Cataloging-in-publication data is available from the Library of Congress.

First edition, 2022

10 9 8 7 6 5 4 3 2 1

N⁰ 1

"Thanks, I'm fine here."

"Beer?"

"Yes."

"Budweiser?"

"No, thanks, it tastes like dishwater, as my wife used to say. I'll have a Sapporo."

As soon as I said that, I remembered who he was, and corrected myself:

"My ex-wife, I mean."

Then, I added:

"I hope you didn't call to have my blessing.... You were quite mysterious on the phone."

He waved his hand dismissively. I took a good look at him: early forties, slightly balding academic with the expression of an honest, intelligent dog—I could tell what Alma saw in him: a reliable pet one could count on at the end of a hard day's work.

"OK," I said. "Because, as far as I'm concerned, she and I are history. Or maybe you wanted to see with your own eyes what you're up against. You must know that our lover's past is like an invisible mountain standing between us and them. You know it's there, but you can't give it a shape, you can't touch it. And it drives you crazy. Believe me, I know. So you wanted to see the mountain. Here it is. Take a good look. Keep in mind that I'm fifteen years older than when I met her. I've put on quite a few pounds. And my hair isn't what it used to be. But then, she, very likely, isn't what she used to be, either. Men used to stop in the street to gawk at her. It's not simply that she was beautiful; she looked as if she came from another planet. Does she still have that dreamy look? She used to stare for minutes like that into the distance.... Before our marriage it made me want to hug her, she seemed so vulnerable, but after, well, after, it's all very different. Have you been married before? No? Never?! Well, good luck. Everything that is touching and charming *before* becomes unbearable *after*. I mean, I come home after a day's work, and she's there, in her armchair, staring at the wall. And she isn't staring for ten minutes; she could sit like that for hours. Without moving. No wonder she had an attraction for monks."

"How did the two of you meet?"

"You mean, she never told you the story? Well, then, let me entertain you. At the time I worked as an electrician at the university. One day I got a call to come fix the VCR in the Languages and Literatures Department. The classroom was empty, and the desk in the middle had a TV and a VCR on it. It was a hot day, so, before starting to work, I took off my T-shirt and secured my hair with a bandana. I had shoulder-length hair then, not like now. So, there I was, with one hand inside the TV, the other holding some wires from the VCR, and my chest bare—need I mention that I used to work out every day?—when I heard a voice coming from the other end of the room.

It was the voice of someone who had just woken up, sleepy and hoarse, vaguely masculine, coming from far away. It scared the bejesus out of me.

"'Jesus,' I said. 'Who's there?'

"The next thing I saw was a wild mesh of long, spiraling dark hair rising above a desk and a creature getting up and moving toward me with the superb idleness of a jungle queen, carrying all that hair on her shoulders and on her back, all the way down to her waist. She came up to me, and I could see that her eyes, dark as her hair, had a spark that reminded me of one of those tribal people seen on National Geographic.

"'I think I fell asleep,' she said. 'Did the class end?'

"'The class? Which class?'

"'French 202. Are you the teacher?'

"'Me?'

"For a second it crossed my mind to say, yes, yes, I'm the teacher. I am whoever you want me to be. Instead, I said:

"'No, nooo…. I'm the electrician.' And I pointed apologetically at the machines on the desk.

"'Oh,' she said. 'I guess that's why you go around bare-chested. It must be part of the job description.'

"She didn't sound sleepy any longer, and was sizing me up quite shamelessly. I told you that at the time I worked out every day, didn't I? Pushups and weights, at least an hour a day. There was plenty to look at, if I may say so myself.

"'What's your name?' I asked.

"'Alma.'

"'*Alma*?! As in *soul*?'

"'Yes, but don't be fooled. It's a misleading name. I have no soul.'

"'Of course you don't. You can't have what you are.'

"In retrospect, I have to agree with her—about the soul. I suppose *you* don't agree with me—yet. Just you wait until you're married."

"I'm not so sure *there will be* a marriage," the man replied, and I noticed, for the first time, how dismal he looked.

"May I ask what happened? I don't want to pry, but since you invited me ..."

He then began to babble in the most incongruous way, so I had to ask him to calm down because I couldn't understand a thing. "What do you mean I'm the only one who can help you?" I asked, but instead of clarifying things, he grew even more confused and confusing. Of that gibberish, all I got was that, as "No.1," I was the only one who could help him. Eventually, it dawned on me that Alma called me No.1 because I had been her first husband.

"Ha! Well, I guess that's better than being No. 2 or 3. Is that what she calls the other two?"

"Yes," he confirmed.

"No, really?! I suppose that would make you No. 4. That is, if ... But I don't understand how *I* can help you. I haven't seen Alma in ages."

He explained—if that stammered mumble could be called an explanation—that what I knew about Alma could "shed some light on the mystery of her disappearance" and help him in his search.

"If you say so.... I'm not one to believe in revelation through words, though."

"What do you mean?"

"I mean that one can talk about something until the cows come home, but it doesn't follow that things are any clearer just because we wrap a lot of words around them; if anything, that should obscure them even more. Talk is the superstition of our times, and everyone believes in it."

"Have you read Freud?"

"Have *I* read Freud? Of course I've read Freud. You people in academia think one needs a degree in order to read anything. And I had my share of academic study, too. Two years in college was all I could take. It was after we got married."

"Was it Alma who wanted you to go to college?"

"No. It was chance. About six months into our marriage I got caught by the campus police smoking pot, and I was fired. One joint and I got the boot. Speaking of which, you wouldn't happen to have a cigarette with you, by any chance, would you? I just finished mine."

He didn't, but a sickly-looking fellow with an unshaved mug who was seated at a nearby table (kind of made you want to quit smoking just by looking at him) did, and he generously offered me one.

"So then, I thought, why not try college? I was still young, twenty-six years old. There was still time to become a physician. That had been my dream ever since I'd been a kid. Plus, I like change. Alma used to say that I had the attention span of a two-year-old. That was *after* the marriage; *before*, she admired me for not dwelling for too long on anything. She said she was happy I wasn't like one of those professors who spend their entire lives writing articles on 'The economy of frustrated desire in the footnotes to the posthumous works of Whatshisname …' Frustrated footnotes, my foot! Of course, later, she would have liked me to become one of those professors. Her chief complaint was that I kept changing my mind and couldn't stick to a choice. It's true that I switched majors a few times. I started with biology because that's what my student advisor suggested, but then, when I saw how many courses were offered and how infinite the possibilities were, as they say in those uplifting commercials, I thought, *Why confine myself to something so narrow?* So, I changed my major to philosophy, because that has always been my natural inclination. And I would have stuck to it, but one of my professors convinced me that I had a mind for political science, and what can one do with a major in philosophy, anyhow? So I switched to political science. Have you ever met a student in political science?"

He shook his head.

"Well, I have, and you wouldn't believe it, these people haven't heard of books. I mean, all they read is articles, and now and then a bestseller by some politician. I was suffocating. I thought, what's the closest field to political science in which people are a little more literary? So, I switched to journalism. Little did I know that … Yes, thank you, I'll have another beer. Well, long story short, journalism didn't work out either, so I moved on to anthropology. By then, Alma had turned into Socrates' wife, if you know what I mean, nagging me all day long, blah-blah-blah, nonstop. You'd never imagine, looking at that royal face of hers, what depths of vitriol are hidden behind it. I'm sorry to shatter your illusions like this, but you'll thank me later. I'm telling you this just so you know what you're getting into. I told you, she and I are history. I know you don't believe me a hundred percent, but it's the truth. No, don't deny it, I've been there. Besides, given her record, I can't blame you for being suspicious. I wouldn't trust her for a second. Even now, when I think of the Monk, and what an idiot I was, I feel like punching him. Did she ever tell you what an ugly trick they played on me?"

Silence, then, that same motion of the head: *no.*

"No, hard to believe! Could it be that she isn't very proud of what she did?

"It was the first summer after she graduated, and she wanted to go to Europe. Of course I wanted to go, too, but at the time I was in a tight spot. I had just started a business and had gotten a loan, and was a little nervous about spending too much on a vacation."

"What business?"

"Well, that's another story. I'm not sure it would interest you."

But he insisted, so I told him the story. About a year earlier I had dropped out of school. School had been a waste of time, and I came to realize I wasn't going anywhere with it. What good is a diploma, anyway? I had worked as an electrician for five years without any certificate or training and did just fine. True, I almost got electrocuted a few times and, at the beginning, every time I repaired something I'd get a call two days later because the damn thing had broken again—little did they know that it had never been fixed in the first place—but, you wouldn't believe it, no one suspected a thing. And you know why? Because people are so trustful in the order of things it would never cross their minds that someone might want to break the rules just for fun. If someone tells you they are an electrician or a plumber, you trust that they are, indeed, an electrician or a plumber. I am not using the word "plumber" gratuitously—I worked as a plumber, too.

Long story short, at the time I was no longer an electrician. Or a student. As I said, I had started a business, a funeral home. I have always been fascinated with the way people deal with death. As a matter of fact, I had done quite extensive research on the topic, and at some point I was even thinking about writing a book. Did he know that in Romania there is a village, Sapînza, whose cemetery, called "The Merry Cemetery," makes fun of death? He didn't. All the tombstones are inscribed with rhymed epigraphs supposedly honoring the deceased, when, in fact, they are making fun of them. Listen to this:

"Here lies a troubled fellow,
A mentally disturbed Othello."
Or:
"His flask was closer to his heart
Then any friend or a beloved."

I thought I could adapt the spirit of Sapînza to our desire for a clean death—"aseptic," as Alma used to say—and use it in a way that would make people feel less frightened by death. All modern societies are afraid of death, but they exorcise their fear in different ways. Our way of exorcising it is by pretending it doesn't exist, when, in fact, the only fact that matters in life is death. It's our only certainty. So, I modeled my funeral home on this idea, and called it "The Joy of Dying." You know, as a counterpoint to *joie de vivre*." I painted the walls of our lobby a bright turquoise, like in Mexican crafts, and put knickknacks on display, including skulls and skeletons of brides and grooms in wedding attire. And a few quotes about death on the walls from Montaigne, Shakespeare, and the like.

At the beginning, there were quite a few journalists who came by and wrote articles about us, and that brought some customers in, but not for long. Most of the time the only people that came in were the curious kind, folks who just wanted to see with their own eyes what they'd read in the papers, as if we were a museum, not a business.

"What did Alma think of all this?"

"By that time," I said, "our relationship had gotten pretty sour. She, generally, has a negative attitude, as you may know by now. She would always emphasize the negative side of things. When I showed her the finished lobby, she pointed out that we still didn't have a place to cremate the bodies, as if I didn't know that. But I wanted us to be more than just a place that would dispose of corpses; I wanted us to offer a space for celebration. So, I designed a wake room where the embalmed corpse would be placed so the family and friends could see it one last time as they celebrated the life of the deceased with champagne and appetizers. I painted that room a peach color with a narrow frieze under the ceiling reproducing medieval images of Hell. I thought it was funny, but apparently not everyone thought so. You can't make fun of Hell in this country. How could you when eighty percent of people believe in angels? I'm not sure what the percentage of people who believe in the Devil is, but it's probably lower. Alma didn't think it was funny either. She doesn't believe in angels, but she does believe in the Devil."

Somewhat impatient, the man asked me to return to the story about Alma and her vacation. I explained that she'd wanted to spend the whole summer in France visiting monasteries. Actually, she'd gotten the idea from me: the previous summer we'd been together in France for about ten days, and since we were very low on cash, I suggested we sleep in monasteries. I asked the man if he'd ever done that. He hadn't. It's really a cheap way of traveling, I said, since most French monasteries have an adjacent building where they host tourists for a small fee, and for another fee they feed you, too. The level of comfort and the quality of the food vary, depending on the place. Some are like youth hostels, others like two-star hotels. Some accept either women or men, and others, both, but again, it depends on the place and the religious order. The Benedictines are the most welcoming. If you can convince them that you are a young soul seeking spiritual nourishment, they will let you sleep in the convent itself and eat with them. You have to attend all that religious spectacle of course, five or six times a day, or however many times a day they pray and sing: *laudes* at daybreak, *messe* at noon, *vêpres* in the afternoon, and *complies* after dinner.

"Thanks," I said to the waiter who had approached. "I'll have another beer. Same, yes."

"What's the name of the place?" asked the man.

"Which place?"

"The monastery."

"Oh … Vézelay. It's, actually, a basilica about two hours and a half from Paris. Vé-ze-lay. Doesn't it sound like a bell—a long drawn-out sound across the grassland in the countryside? You can visualize the cows moving slowly under the gradually setting sun with their bells jingling: vé-ze-lay, vé-ze-lay. And yet there weren't any cows there. It was a small town, not a village. The main street crossed the entire town, sloping upward alongside boutiques, restaurants, and wine-tasting rooms. It was the end of June when we went there, but it felt like fall, and we couldn't stop shivering in our light summer clothes.

* * *

When we set out to explore the town there were only a few tourists ambling along purposelessly, like us, most of them old. A wine tasting room with its doors opened seemed to invite us inside, so we went in. There was no one there. The room was cool, and its white walls were covered with wine racks storing dozens of bottles. In the center was a large, heavy walnut table with two bottles on it—one of white and one of red wine— and two glasses. There was something monastic about the whole setting, in spite of the obvious pleasure-seeking goal behind it. Maybe it was the white silence permeating everything, or maybe the vague feeling that the ultimate aim here was not pleasure itself but the submission to some kind of age-old ritual. The bottles and the glasses stood there expectant—they were *expecting* us. We called out to indicate our presence, saying *Hello* and *Bonjour,* and then, again, *Helloooo,* but there was no answer. Alma wanted to leave, but I was no fool. I proceeded immediately to reendow the bottles and glasses with their original purpose by pouring half a glass of white into one and half of red into another. I don't know whether it was the secret pleasure of consuming something that wasn't ours, or whether that wine was touched by divine grace, but never have I tasted anything close to it, neither before nor after. It tasted like nectar stolen from the gods. As the liquid traveled from your mouth to your stomach, your body was filled with a tangy sweetness when tasting the red, and a dry coolness when tasting the white. It was in drinking that wine that I understood what communion must really mean for those who believe in it. I felt as if my body was losing its outline, spilling into the outside world, and the outside world was pouring all its contents into my expanding body. When we finished those bottles, I began to explore the rows of wine along the walls, but Alma, who could cool off a volcano with her calculating and controlling mind, insisted that we leave.

"Can't you see that we were invited here by a higher order?" I asked.

"Since when do you believe in a higher order?"

We were both a little unstable on our feet, but, luckily, the table was there for us.

"One doesn't find such wine twice in a lifetime. We can't just walk away!"

"Can't you just enjoy something, and stop like a normal person when you reach your limit?"

"Maybe *you*'ve reached your limit. I haven't."

"Fine, you can stay here and I'll go. But I'm not going to bail you out if they throw you in jail. Besides, there is plenty of wine in the *hôtellerie*'s cellar."

As she walked out the door, I thought that maybe she was right, after all. To be honest, it was the thought that our *hôtellerie*—that's how they called the place where we stayed, "a guest house"—stood on top of a wine cellar that convinced me to abandon the wine tasting room, but not before I grabbed a dusty bottle of red from a nearby shelf. Alma was already about fifty feet away when I stepped out holding the bottle and shaking on my feet. I called her, but she refused to answer. The sun had already set, and the main street was almost deserted, so I wasn't afraid of witnesses, and I kept calling her name, Almaaaaa … She pretended she didn't know me, so we both zigzagged our way up that slope, all the way to the top at the *hôtellerie*. By the time I arrived there it was already dark, and I found her waiting for me with that grin of an unsatisfied wife that was now her default expression.

Our room was on the fourth floor of the *hôtellerie*, an old edifice adjacent to the twelve-century basilica of Sainte Madeleine, with long corridors whose walls of compact gray stone kept the air cool at all times. Besides the coiling stairs between the floors, there was nothing distinctive about the building. The toilet we were told to use was opposite our room, which would have been quite comfortable had it not been for the wave of cold air that hit you when you opened the door. The room itself was small and very much like a dorm room, with the beds so narrow that if you moved you fell on the floor. Actually, that night I *did* fall at least twice. And if you wonder whether my wife came to my rescue, no, she didn't move a finger.

"I hope you broke something," she mumbled.

Yes, that's what my wife said. But the next morning I was as good as new, I just had a bad aftertaste in my mouth, as if I'd eaten dog meat, while she, on the other hand, could barely stand up. I let her go to the basilica to attend the religious service and repent, and I went looking for Frère Ivan—our *hôtelier*—to ask him to give me a tour. At first he was apprehensive—he even mentioned a robbery that had happened not long ago— but when I told him I was a student in European history and was writing a paper on French monastic life, he mellowed and agreed to the tour.

Frère Ivan wasn't very talkative. As we made our way down the stairs, I did all the talking, hoping that if I drowned him in my babble, he wouldn't have time to get suspicious and change his mind. When we finally reached the first floor, I asked him whether the *Fraternité*—that is, the brothers—produced anything of their own, the way most monasteries do—say, honey, soap, cookies, candies, or … wine. At this, Frère Ivan's face lit up and he began to talk. They produced a spiritual magazine, he said. In fact, they were considering expanding its distribution to their brothers from across the ocean, and they were examining the possibility of having some of the essays translated into English. Was I interested in helping them, by chance?

I swallowed up my deception, but thought that I shouldn't throw away the opportunity to bond with Frère Ivan.

"I'm sure I could help you in some way," I said decisively but vaguely. "Let me think about it."

As I uttered this, I noticed an arched wooden door at the end of the hall, and asked him where it led.

"It's the door to our cellar," he answered casually, and was about to move on.

"Oh, the cellar. That reminds me … Part of my paper is about the monks' domestic life and, come to think of it, it would be quite interesting to include the cellar in it. Would you mind …?"

Frère Ivan made a gesture as if to indicate that he didn't care one way or another, though he didn't understand why anyone would be interested in something as innocuous as a cellar. At the door, he pulled his ring of keys out of the large pocket of his ankle-long cassock. It was a huge ring with maybe fifteen keys on it, some of them three inches long. After he found the key to the cellar, and the door opened with a long screech, we descended the three or four uneven stairs at the entrance. The only source of light came from the open door, so we had to make an effort to see. It was even colder there than in the rest of the building, yet, as soon as I stepped in, I felt my body opening up to a hospitable warmth. I have no idea how many bottles could have been in there, but there were a lot more than in that tasting room. It was a small, uninviting space with parallel rows of wine racks dividing it like cubicles in an office, with the bottles, old and covered with dust, popping out of them, waiting to be plucked like ripe fruit. There were cobweb laces running between the racks, and the air was damp and stale. And yet stepping in there felt like coming *home*. I could have stayed there forever, inhaling that stale air and touching those ... those holy chalices in which blood-thick, fermented grape juices had been poured and transubstantiated into a divine elixir. We stayed there for less than a minute, but it was long enough to notice a smaller, wooden door at the other end, through which a ray of light came in.

"Could we go out through that door?" I asked.

"No. That opens onto the garden."

As soon as we were out of there and Frère Ivan locked the door, I let him go back to his monkish ways, and I went straight to the kitchen. I took a corkscrew and a flashlight, and for a second I considered also grabbing a glass, but in the end I decided against it. With the corkscrew in my pocket and the flashlight in my right hand, I exited the *hôtellerie* and followed its angular outline until I found myself in the unkempt garden behind it. There was a big chestnut tree in the middle with a bench underneath and a cobblestone path starting next to it, snaking its way between grass and some pale, withered flowers. I spotted the little wooden door behind a flight of stairs leading down. I was prepared to face resistance and was already imagining various ways of forcing the door, when I noticed a latch in the upper right side. I barely touched it, and the door opened almost gracefully, with no resistance at all. I turned on the flashlight and stepped inside, closing the door behind me. I hadn't experienced such an exhilarating feeling since I'd been a child, engaged in mischief with the other boys in the neighborhood. Patches of light moved jerkily from rack to rack, following my nervous movements. I decided I first needed to create my setting, and began to look for something on which to sit. Eventually, I found a small wooden crate with empty bottles in it, took the bottles out, and used it as a chair. Now, the fun could begin. The Search. The search for what? For the Holy Grail, of course. For the bottle that among all those dozens or hundreds of bottles contained in it that divine combination of grapes, Time and Sun, in perfect proportion. I was in no hurry, so I spent about an hour examining dozens of bottles, and reading their yellowed labels on which someone had written, with a ballpoint pen, "Merlot, 1979," "Cabernet Sauvignon, 1985," "Pinot Noir, 1975." It was a 1985 Pinot Noir that I ended up choosing, and I wasn't sorry, though it didn't equal the experience from the day before. All the same, the hours spent in that dark, cavernous space, surrounded by cobwebs and spooky shadows, were among the best in my life. I've had quite a bit of fun in my life, but, believe me, nothing compares with an exquisite bottle of wine, and when I say, "exquisite,"

I don't mean something you can find in a supermarket or the neighborhood liquor store.

After I finished the Pinot Noir, I consulted my watch and saw that it was well past dinner time. Alma was surely wondering where I was. I considered going to our room and inviting her to my hiding place, but realized immediately that she wouldn't go for it. She would very likely get hysterical, I thought, and threaten to tell on me. Better to take advantage of the situation on my own. So I opened a second bottle. By the time I finished, it was very late, and going back to the room no longer seemed like an option. Besides, I was quite comfortable in my new surroundings in spite of the lack of furniture. True, my chair was a little austere, but with my jacket on it, it felt almost soft. My eyes had gotten used to the dark, and I could easily find my way around. The bottles now seemed like lost friends I had rediscovered after we'd been separated and gone our own ways, and my eyes teared up at the sight of them. In fact, my strained eyes spotted, cuddled up in a corner, my best childhood friend, Mike, the same as he was when I'd last seen him. I opened my arms and walked toward him, drunk with happiness. I hugged him and hugged him until he got tired of my grip, and vanished. Then I grew sad, very sad, and opened a third bottle, aware all the while that someone—but who? I couldn't remember— was waiting for me. This knowledge gnawed at me, though it was a muddled awareness, only strong enough to stop me from thoroughly enjoying myself. And then I fell asleep.

When I woke up, I was lying on the cement floor. A ray of pale light was struggling to peek through the small wooden door. I looked at my watch—7:30. I must have slept there all night, I thought, and tried to get up. My body hurt as if I'd been splitting wood for a week or had been training for the Olympics, or as if a housewife had hammered it like a piece of raw meat. I stood up, wailing in pain, picked up all the incriminating evidence— the corkscrew, the flashlight, and my jacket—and left.

In our room, Alma was still asleep. I knelt before her bed and kissed her hand. She twitched and turned on her back, then slowly opened her eyes. They were red and swollen, as if she'd been crying. I began my apology, "I'm sorry...." She blinked, raised her head all the while massaging it with her right hand, propped her back on the pillow and, adjusting her body to a comfortable sitting position, gazed at me through half-closed eyes, as if I were a worm she was about to crush. "You pig...." she began. "I'm sorry," I repeated. "You animal...." And before I could say again, "I'm sorry," I felt a shower of small fists all over my body. I let her get it out of her system, and then tried to get my side of the story in.

We left Vézelay later that day.

"But what was the point of telling you all this? Oh, yes, how Alma got the idea to spend a whole summer in French monasteries. That was the next summer."

"Would you like another beer?" he asked.

"Sure.... I'll have whatever you have—as long as it isn't Budweiser.

"Yes, the next summer. I could tell she was happy to go by herself, and, frankly, I wasn't too upset, either, we both needed some time away from each other. Plus, I wanted to concentrate on my funeral home business, and figure out a way to move forward. Yes, the next summer Alma went back to France by herself, and wrote me long letters that I read so many times I knew them by heart; not that I missed her, no ... Rather, I had a foreboding; I could tell something was in store for me, I could smell it between the lines full of detailed descriptions of the monasteries, the abbeys, and the nuns, descriptions on which I gorged with the sick joy of a patient who knows he has cancer and wants the doctor to confirm he's right."

She began her trip, I recounted, with the Monastery of the Immaculate Conception in Rouen. Aren't these Catholics funny? The "Monastery of the Immaculate Conception." It would have been even more ironic if she had met *him* there—but no. It wasn't there. This was a convent—Benedictines. I don't know what she told them, but they let her sleep in the cloister. She probably pretended to be Catholic, though I'm sure she didn't fool anyone. I don't think she even knows how to make the sign of the cross properly. Well, maybe by now she knows, after having been married to a monk, but at the time, when she attended mass, and the priest distributed the communion wafers to the faithful, and it was her turn, she just stood there, watching his hand move higher and higher with the wafer further and further from her mouth, and the hand's owner increasingly irritated. "May God be with you!" he said, as he watched her with expectant eyes. She too watched him, with her mouth open, having the confusing feeling that he was expecting an answer from her. Exasperated, she said, "OK, then," grabbed the wafer from his hand, and placed it in her mouth. Then, pushing aside the wine chalice—she wasn't going to drink from the same receptacle dozens of other mouths had drunk from—she turned her back on him and left.

She narrated this anecdote in her first letter, speculating that she must have done something wrong, because the priest's eyes were shooting daggers. But in spite of this inauspicious beginning, she attended almost all the religious services for a whole week, even the *laudes*. And she isn't an early riser, to put it mildly. When we were together, there were days when she'd get up at eleven. I asked him if she still had the same morning habits, and, not surprisingly, he confirmed that yes, she had. People change less than one might think.

At any rate, at the monastery she did her best to change. She had always claimed—laughing—that her true vocation was a monastic life. I think her "vocation" was more like a devilish perversity, the perversity that inspired her to seduce a man who had devoted his life to God.

At this point he interrupted me, remarking in a rather quarrelsome tone that it was not *she* who'd seduced him.

"What are you?" I asked, without even trying to conceal my scorn. "A child? A fool? Of course *she* seduced him, and if she told you otherwise, she's a liar, and you are ... But, after all, what do *I* care? It's *your* life.

"Where was I? Yes, the Monastery of the Immaculate Conception. The nuns gave Alma a small room in the cloister, similar to the one we had in Vézelay, only warmer, with the toilet and the shower next door. The room was equipped with a rundown table on which a Bible and a sheet with the hours of religious service had been placed, and a crucifix above the table, exactly as in our room in Vézelay. What was different was the monastery's *produit d'artisanat*, that is, the craft the nuns specialized in! And as luck would have it, the Benedictines of the Immaculate Conception specialized in *madeleines*—you know, that delicate, leaf-shaped shortcake from Proust that has the gift of bringing back memories. In fact, the main reason Alma— with whose sweet tooth you may be familiar—had chosen this monastery was the madeleines. She spent about three hours a day in the basement with the nuns packing madeleines in little plastic bags tied up with golden ribbons, and you can imagine that some of those treats were sacrificed every now and then to her impatient palate. The entire building—and it was an enormous, old one, dating back to the seventeenth-century—was constantly suffused with vanilla and powdered sugar aromas.

"I still have the letters Alma sent me from there, which I remember quite well, and there is one in which she describes the sensuousness resulting from the contrast between the lightness of the sweet vanilla scent and the heaviness of the gray, cold slabs. I could picture her lingering in those halls and touching the stone with the reverence of a pilgrim who fetishizes nuns' clothing. Those halls, by the way, were part of a rectangle; that is, the building was in the shape of a rectangle with its front side missing, and a flight of spiral stairs at each corner of the rectangle. I assume the design was clear and logical, but Alma, whose lack of a sense of direction you must be familiar with, felt as if she were in a labyrinth, and claimed that you could start using the flight of stairs at one end, and then, if you chose to cross the hall of a given floor, and then used the flight of stairs at the other end, you ended up moving in circles, as if the building were round. If she *really* moved in circles, then the building must have had also a front side; but if it didn't have one, as she claims, then one can only move in circles if one turns around in the same spot—which she may have very well done, since once she spent an hour in a parking lot looking for her car.

"But Alma does have a particular sensitivity when it comes to touching and smelling, which was very likely at the root of her monastic phase," I added.

"I don't think it was simply a phase...." (the same antagonistic tone).

"You mean she still goes to monasteries?"

"Temples. Japanese temples."

"Well, all the more reason to call it a phase. But one can't deny that she's perseverant: for a whole week, armed with a

Bible in one hand and a songbook in the other—in French, no less—she sang with the sisters, who chanted, I believe, in the Gregorian tradition. In another one of her letters she gave me a long lesson on the specifics that give monastic chanting that otherworldly quality—for there is no doubt that its sustained monotone 'takes one to a realm of mental peace akin to the sky's pale blue, a realm with no passion and no pain.' There was a time when I knew by heart Alma's description of the sisters' chanting. I still remember the songs because she brought back a tape purchased in the abbey's shop, and in the first weeks after her return I had to listen to it over and over. She pointed out that while most music stirs and exacerbates our passions, and thus unsettles us, Gregorian music acts in the opposite way, quieting us down and soothing our senses, but not the way New Age music, for instance, does it. The latter imitates natural sounds and tries to reproduce nature's peacefulness, while monastic music takes us away from nature, it lifts us to a place where nature doesn't exist, where *we* don't exist, and once we are up there, it proceeds to shake off the world like a shell of extraneous clutter, relieving us of our bodies and the objects that surround us, until all that remains is the world before creation, pure, light, and even. It is this evenness that, according to Alma, Gregorian music expresses. Well, I was never quite so taken by it as her, but I have to admit that it does calm one down—although in my case it ended up having the opposite effect. For years, after she left me for the Monk, the simple mention of Gregorian music made my blood pressure go up.

"I can picture my Alma—sorry, did I say, '*my* Alma'? I mean, *our* Alma, of course—seated on one of those uncomfortable wooden benches, eyes closed, livid forehead raised toward the arched ceiling, nostrils dilated by the burning incense, senses opened to that unadorned Paradise of unmoved stone. I think

Alma is an aesthete of space, which is why she ended up marrying an architect—Number 3."

"Speaking of No. 3, I am really worried because of him."

"You mean that not everything is over between the two of them?"

"I'm afraid he might do something stupid. You know he's very jealous."

"So I've been told."

* * *

One week with the immaculate nuns of Rouen: it would have driven me crazy. Not Alma. She used to say, "My dear, if you didn't manage to drive me crazy, no one will!" After Rouen, Alma returned to Paris, and, a short train ride from there, to the Abbey Notre-Dame de Jouarre. Rouen had been sunk in grayness and covered by a veil of cold drizzle, as Normandy always is, so it was a relief to see the abbey with its surrounding edifices shine in the warm June light. The monastic domain of Jouarre is one of the biggest in France, and in the postcards reproducing it from above, like this one (I took the postcard from my pocket), one can see several big rectangles: in the back, at the left, the old Roman Tower and the church; at the right, the cloister, with its three sides enclosing the garden, and a glass enclosure on the first floor, like a hothouse or a glass verandah covering the cloister's full length. The fourth side of the rectangle, the one in front, is the back wall of one of the guest dorms. Though Benedictines, the nuns of Jouarre don't accept anyone inside the cloister, but they have more than enough space for guests and tourists—at least two very large buildings. The other guest dorm is at the left, right behind the abbey—"see this building? No, the other one, in the foreground. You may keep the postcard, I brought it for you.

"It was at Jouarre that Alma met the woman who would end up changing both our lives: Patrice," I concluded. "Have you met Patrice?"

He hadn't.

"But you must know who she is. After she got married to the Monk, Alma used me for a while as her confidant, and Patrice was at the top of her complaints' list. 'A jealous sister with a ...' How did she put it? '... with a perverted Electra complex, in which her brother has replaced the father figure'... or something like that. It was Patrice who invited Alma to the Saint-Martin Monastery in Ligugé, where she used to go every summer to see her brother. As in all the stories with a good punch line, Alma declined. At first."

* * *

After a week at Jouarre, Alma took the train back to Paris, and from there again to morose Normandy at the *Monastère de la Visitation* in Caen, an order of the *Visitandines* nuns, and don't ask me in what way they are different from the Benedictines. Even the buildings' colors matched the weather: while the domain of Jouarre was painted a joyful light cream with red roofs, the one in Caen was a cold gray with dark blue roofs. The postcards sent by Alma represented similar architectural styles for the main buildings, even though the Jouarre Abbey is much older. The reason may be because the main buildings' façades in both places go back to the eighteenth and the nineteenth-centuries, respectively, while other parts are from various other periods. The Roman Tower in Jouarre, for instance, is from the twelfth century, I believe. At any rate, it seems to me that the traditional style of most French monasteries is that of a rectangle with one of its sides missing. Another characteristic is that one of the three sides has another wing built perpendicular to it somewhere in the middle. Some monasteries and abbeys have a crypt with relics of saints, like the one in Caen. Needless to say, the sisters are very proud of these relics.

One night, Alma called me from Caen. It was really late, maybe two in the morning. She was crying. She said she was sick of monasteries and boring nuns, and tired of carrying suitcases, of taking the train and waiting for taxis in the rain, and she wanted to come home. And guess what I said? Ha, ha! Guess what I said? I said, don't be silly, sweetheart, you just need to rest, and tomorrow everything will be all right again. And then I said, why don't you call that woman, Patrice, and arrange to spend some time with her? Yes, that's what I said. Isn't life a joke? Who knows, if I hadn't said that, we might still be married today. If I hadn't said that, we might not be here today because Alma would still be my wife.

"I wouldn't count on that," the weasel mumbled. I was pondering what the appropriate response to that was—to ignore him or punch him in the nose—when he began to rant against "brides who run away before the wedding" and "women one can't trust," and then he asked:

"How can a woman disappear just like that without a word?"

I was beginning to suspect that there was something more there.

"What woman are you talking about?"

"What woman? Alma, of course. Who else?"

"You mean, she's disappeared?"

"Disappeared. Vanished. Gone."

Little by little I got out of him that Alma had gone away without a word about a week earlier, and he still hadn't heard from her. She'd done that before, but not for longer than two or three days.

"Why didn't you say anything so far?! Have you talked to Nora?"

No, he hadn't talked to Nora, he wanted to see me first. I told him that she was the one he should talk to.

"Well, I guess that's the end of my story," I added. "The next day Alma called Patrice, and then went to that monastery near Poitiers where she met the Monk. And one year later we were divorced.

"What more do you want to hear? OK, I'll tell you more, if that's what you want. Yes, I'll have another beer.

"Alma never told me what happened at the Abbey of St. Martin in Ligugé. Nora did. Of course, I myself met the Monk a year later. Nora claims that at the time the Monk looked like a cross between Richard Burton and Christopher Reeve. Maybe that's how women saw him. Personally, the only thing I saw was those intense blue eyes. Otherwise, he was rather unremarkable and definitely in need of a good workout. The most interesting thing that Nora said was what had triggered Alma's interest— because you always wonder, what, why? She said that when Patrice introduced them, Alma was intrigued by the Monk's indifference. Like all beautiful women, she was used to being looked at, and the Monk was the first man she'd ever met— besides the gay ones, of course—who seemed utterly unmoved by her charms. Not only that, but he practically looked *through* her, as if he didn't really see her. It was as if he belonged to a different race. He lived in a different realm, and in that realm her power was cancelled.

"Alma, as you probably know, is very stubborn and curious. She cannot accept that something might be beyond her grasp, and seeing that she had no power over this man—something in itself incomprehensible—she proceeded to use all the weapons at her disposal to make sure her power hadn't disappeared. Of course, I'm only speculating, but I'm pretty sure I'm right. Nora put it differently. She said that what Alma wanted was to understand the essence of that Other Power the Monk had given himself to, a power so strong it annihilated her own. I don't know how long it took her to claim victory, whether he acted like an innocent lamb she just led by the nose, or whether he participated willingly in the charade, pretending to explain the abbey's history to his guest—there was plenty to explain, after all, as St. Martin de Ligugé is the oldest monastery in the Western world. She stayed there for almost a month, and after that phone call, all I received from her was this postcard—yes, you may keep this one, too—and a letter in which she described in great detail all the nooks and crannies of the new place, but not a word about the monks. I've learned a lot about the double cloister and the abbey's architecture, if you're interested. The cloister, by the way, is the long hall linking the various parts of an abbey. You can see that this one is 'double' because it's divided into two lanes by a row of stone columns, which crosses the hall from one end to the other, where a wooden Christ agonizes eternally on the wall, and from there to another, perpendicular end with yet another agonizing Christ. The stone columns, whose upper parts fan out toward the arched ceiling, run alongside the huge windows facing the inner courtyard, through which one can see the well-kept garden with its trimmed bushes and shrubs, as the sun penetrating through the windowpanes casts shadows of the pale columns on the floor's pastel tiles. In this hall one occasionally spots the gray, rushed fluttering of a monk's cloak on his way to his cell or the church. So, are you going to ask me if this is where my wife and her Monk met every day for a whole month? Frankly, I have no idea. But I can imagine him telling her stories about Saint Martin, how Saint Martin had come to that very spot almost a thousand six hundred years ago to be a hermit, and then a basilica was built, and then destroyed, in the good old European tradition, and then rebuilt around the year one thousand. And like all the other cathedrals, monasteries, and abbeys, this one too went through its periods of enlargement, shrinking, additions, and other changes over the centuries. The double cloister is, apparently, from the nineteenth century. Those who say it's the oldest monastery in the Western world simply mean that somewhere in that construction there is a sixteen-centuries-old stone. It's the same way here when we say that someone is a Native American even if he is only one-sixteenth Native American.

"At any rate, I'm sure this story contributed to Alma's infatuation. Half of 'falling in love' is context. How can you beat a blue-eyed monk hiding in a fourth-century abbey where Rabelais himself had once worked as a secretary for the *prieur*? Well, but none of this makes any difference now. I'm sorry for the Monk, though. He really had it rough. Imagine: sixteen years as a monk, then a woman comes along and steals you away from what was your life's calling, and then, a few years later, she drops you like a hot potato. And for whom? For ... Well, but what's the point of rehashing all this now? Let me finish this beer and I'll take off.

"When Alma returned, it was clear something was going on. She was distant, and soon I noticed that she was receiving mail from France. This was still before email—at least, we didn't have it. And then, one day, no doubt inspired by a story she'd heard from Patrice about how the latter's mother had dumped her husband ('Jacques, I am leeeving you') she greeted me with, 'I'm divorcing you.' Just like that! I'm sure she'd rehearsed that in front of a mirror. I didn't think it was funny. I almost hit her. She may have told you that I broke all the porcelain in the house, but that's not true. I only broke the porcelain we'd received at our wedding. But I would have gladly broken her neck. In the end, she left me and filed for divorce."

"Did you meet the Monk?"

"Yes, sure I did. Maybe I wasn't very ... civil at first. I was still angry, but, eventually, I forgave them. And we—the three of us, I mean—were more or less on friendly terms until that funeral."

"What funeral?"

"You mean she never told you?! Well, that was quite a memorable funeral. It was three years or so after they got married. The Monk's mother—who was also Patrice's mother—died of cancer, and the Monk was devastated. He was incapable of dealing with the funeral himself, so Alma told him not to worry, she'd take care of it. And she came to me, since at the time I still had my funeral business, which was going better than ever. And I said, 'Just leave it to me.' And meant it. I wanted to organize a ceremony that would capture the essence of a person's life in a way that was consistent with the spirit of our enterprise, a way of seeing death not as frightening, but as something one can joke about.

"And so I asked Alma to make me a list of what the deceased had liked most in life, and she did. I remember: snow, cigarettes, twenties' fashion and style, red roses, Gregory Peck, Nat King Cole, a cloudless sky. I painted our event room sky blue with white snowflakes on it, and hung Gregory Peck photographs all over, including one in which we replaced Lana Turner with a young image of the deceased in which she was looking at Greg with sultry eyes and a half-open, glossy-red mouth. I ordered a beautiful oak coffin, lined it with sky-blue silk, and placed the deceased inside. We dressed her in a twenties' black dress with white pearls and a black wig with shoulder-length straight hair and bangs. I placed in her hands, near the heart, a red rose, and wanted to insert a long cigarette in her rouged mouth, but it was hard to open it, so I took out our skeleton—Tim, we called him—and made him stand near the coffin with a cigarette in his grinning mouth, and tied a rose around his genitalia. On the floor, all around Tim and the catafalque, I scattered red rose petals. It was all so cool I almost wished I could change places with the dead woman. Believe me, it was a scene to behold. And then, we placed a table against the Eastern wall, draped it in light blue silk, scattered some more red rose petals on it, and put bowls and plates of humus, bagels, lox, cheese, crackers, and cookies on it. And another table against the Western wall with champagne, red wine, and crystal glasses. It was all very nice, but a little conservative, so we decided to spice it up by hanging strips of colored paper from the ceiling with little plastic skeletons and skulls at their ends. And standing by the door was a young boy with a scythe and a wicker basket full of special-ordered Chinese fortune-cookies, which the guests were supposed to pick up and open to retrieve messages such as 'Next year on this day you'll be struck dead by lightening,' or 'Your daughter will give birth to a three-eyed monster,' or 'Your hemorrhoid will grow as big as an orange,' or 'Your progeny will die of plague and syphilis.' We had a lot of fun with those.... It was our pièce de résistance, but unfortunately our guests didn't seem to appreciate it. Imagine a room swinging in the languid rhythm of Nat King Cole's 'Unforgettable,' and a throng of guests entering with hesitant steps, the way people do in such occasions, as if they were afraid to wake up the deceased, and being offered at the door a fortune cookie, which they take with an intrigued expression. Imagine these guests walk about under the colored paper with skeletons and skulls, some of them going up to the coffin, others to the Eastern table, and others to the Western table, now and then one of them remembering that they are holding something in their hands, and absentmindedly breaking up the cookie, extracting the tiny white strip of paper, and then hiding it in their pocket with an expression of utter bafflement. Oh, those faces! You should have seen those faces reading those fortune cookies! It was truly unforgettable.

"The problem was that the Monk didn't have a sense of humor. He entered the room grave and stern, holding his fortune cookie away from his body, as if afraid of being contaminated, and, as he took in the scene around him, his face grew progressively dark and his body stiffened. Then, he advanced toward the casket with his eyes wide open as if about to pop out, kneeled in front of the catafalque, took the wig from the deceased's head, and threw it on the floor in anger. All the whispers and the murmurs in the room ceased, as everyone watched in silence. He then attempted to lift the corpse, but without much success, and, with a voice strangled by fury, asked for help. Someone rushed to help him, and together they carried the corpse toward the door. In the ensuing commotion and confusion, some of the guests left, expressing their outrage in low voices, while others stayed without daring to move, as if hypnotized. I saw Alma run up to the Monk and whisper something in his ear.

"'I won't allow my mother's body to be desecrated!' he yelled.

"'But you can't take it out in the sun!' she pleaded.

"In the end, she convinced him to bring the corpse back to the catafalque and to clean up the room. They took down all the Gregory Peck photographs, and relieved poor Tim of his rose and cigarette. By the time they finished, most of the guests were gone. Alma gave me a look; you know, one of those looks. We didn't speak for years after that. They never paid for all the expenses I'd incurred. The Monk sent me a check for about a third of the bill, and a note saying I should count myself lucky he wasn't suing me. The unpaid bill was the last drop in the full glass of debts I had, and soon afterward, 'The Joy of Dying' folded.

"Well, time for us to go now. Looks like this place is closing."

N<u>o</u>. 2

I invited him to sit down and offered him some Merlot. I happened to have a bottle from a very good year. Did he mind if I put some music on? No, he didn't. Before his arrival I had been listening to Mendelssohn's *Violin Concerto in E Minor*, one of my favorite violin concertos. For some reason, whenever I listen to this piece I think back to the time when I was living in a monastery, maybe because of the type of passion summoned by the violin's anguished sound, a different passion than ordinary, earthbound emotion. The latter is a two-way street: even if you suffer of unrequited love, you still receive something from the object of your love. Even if what you receive is hatred, you still are in an emotional relationship. But the passion I am talking about, the one I hear in Mendelssohn's violin, is pure because it takes you to a different world, it reminds me of the feeling one can experience only in a monastic cell. There, your senses are channeled toward a higher plane, and you are nothing but a vessel longing for it.

I realized I was thinking out loud and asked him to excuse me.

"You have to tell me again how you think I can help you because on the phone it wasn't quite clear. I understand that your wedding to Alma is … *was* supposed to take place in a month, and she disappeared two weeks ago. Now, please explain what you mean by 'disappeared'."

"Disappeared—as in she left without any warning or any note, and nobody knows where. She did take a suitcase of clothes with her."

"Yes, this *is* strange … Hard to say … Where could she have gone? May I ask if there were any disagreements between the two of you prior to her disappearance? Was there anything that could have made her break off the engagement?"

"No, nothing. At least, not as far as I could tell. Maybe I didn't know her well enough. That's why I wanted to talk to you. Is she very unpredictable?"

"Hmm, she certainly acted unpredictably with *me!* How do you like the wine? But, please, sit down! Walking in circles isn't going to help."

The man, who informed me that Alma liked to call him "No. 4," was very agitated and, in spite of my repeated attempts to get him to sit down, continued to stand and move about. After several minutes of pacing to and fro, he stopped abruptly and asked me if I had any misgivings about him. I reassured him that he had nothing to worry about.

"In fact, one could say that you restored some kind of balance after you did to the Architect what he'd done to me."

"This is exactly what I'm afraid of."

"Are you saying that he … that he might want to get revenge on you?"

I had to stop the music in order to hear the unintelligible sounds coming from his throat and to concentrate on what he was saying.

"Are you implying there might be a connection between Alma's disappearance and the Architect's jealousy?" I asked. Because, if that's what you're implying, then either Alma has gone back to him, or else ..."

No sooner had I uttered those words than he began to wring his hands and rub his forehead in a gesture of hopelessness, all the while continuing to move about.

"I'm sorry, I didn't want to make you panic, please calm down! Please, I was simply trying to draw some logical conclusions from your words."

"He'd tried to kill her before," he said, and this time I wasn't sure we were still talking about the same person.

"You mean, the Architect?!"

He nodded: yes.

"Before ... when? When they were married? How?"

"He threatened her...."

"Did she tell you why?"

"He was jealous because she'd danced with another man."

Poor Alma, I thought. Then, out of the blue, he asked me if *our* marriage had been "happy." I took a deep breath and thought for a couple of minutes before opening my mouth again.

"At the beginning, the first two years more precisely, we were very happy. At least, I was as happy as is humanly possible. We were poor, living on her small income as a teaching assistant while she was studying for her Master's, yet these were the happiest years of my life. I was still trying to find my place outside the monastery, and didn't have a job. You have to understand that it isn't easy to find work after you lived for sixteen years in a monastery in France. And readapting to the American lifestyle wasn't easy, either. And yet I was happy. I became a housewife, and gladly so. Every day I waited for Alma to come back from school with a set table and dishes simmering on the stove. I learned to prepare all her favorite dishes. I even made her macaroni and cheese. Do you know when I'd eaten macaroni and cheese the last time? When I was ten years old.

"For the first time in my life I was experiencing the joy of eating. At the monastery, food had been only a means of staying alive. I used to eat fast and without paying much attention to what was in front of me. But Alma is a very sensuous eater. The first time I noticed that was when we had a picnic together one afternoon in the monastery's garden. I had brought some soft cheese—I don't recall the brand, but it was probably cow cheese from the region—bread and cider, all in a wicker basket, and we sat down on the grass. I don't remember why my sister wasn't there. The first week after Alma's arrival, she accompanied us everywhere, so she must have had a reason not to be there at the time. It was a warm afternoon, and the bees were particularly excited, getting drunk on the wildflowers around us. Alma screamed whenever one of them was getting too close, so we had to move several times. I was nervous because we were alone. It occurred to me while we sat there in silence that a woman is a creature whose thoughts are impenetrable. We sat like that for minutes without a word, and the more time we spent together, the stranger and more elusive she became. It goes without saying that I hadn't spent much time in the company of women in all those years, and when I did, I didn't think of them as 'women.' For the first time I was alone with a *woman*, and she was as remote and mysterious as a rock. But what was even more mysterious than her existence was the knowledge that she must have the same nervous system as mine, so she too must have had thoughts about me while we both sat there in that ambiguous, awkward silence. Then, we began to eat, and she ate her cheese in a way that made me reconsider that soft, white matter I always ate in a hurry, and which in her mouth turned into some kind of pleasure-triggering device. She ate it very slowly, letting it melt on her tongue, and making now and then some low, moaning sounds. As I watched her eat, I realized for the first time how mysterious a human being—*any* human being—is. The way she chewed and chewed ... I imagined the minced lump of food moving down a tube into her stomach, and that seemed miraculous. Everything about her was miraculous. The way a lock of hair moved on her forehead, or the way the sun rested on her dark hair, surrounding it with a halo of melancholy gold. I couldn't stop staring at her. It was as if I had suddenly become aware of something in the universe that I didn't know existed, and this something had the power of filling with joy anyone in its immediate vicinity. As soon as we separated that day, I felt that all the joy of living was deserting me, as if she possessed a magical object everything inside me desperately needed. I understood then why women had been condemned in the old days for witchcraft: what I felt was exactly what a man upon whom a spell had been cast must have experienced.

"I have been asked after I left the monastery whether in those first days of my infatuation, or at the moment it dawned on me that I had what one might call 'sinful feelings' for a woman, I felt guilty. And people were surprised when I said no, I didn't feel guilty at all. The reason I didn't feel guilty is that, until we kissed, it never occurred to me that something 'wrong' was going on. As I said, I had no experience with women, and aside from a few crushes in my childhood and adolescence, my soul was as much of a blank page as my body. What I was feeling in those first days was, in fact, akin to the elated state I'd known on the rare occasions I experienced the presence of God in my cell. It was the same lightness of being, the same vague dizziness and blurring of vision, until this blurring and this vagueness grew increasingly clearer, and all my senses sharpened, focused on a single, transparent point. But it was rare for that point to reveal itself to me; usually, I was in a state of drunken exhilaration, ready to receive the blessing of celestial bliss every day and every instant.

"One of my favorite places for passing the time was our library, a large room with dark wood floors and shelves brimming with old, yellowed Gallimard editions of the works of Theillard de Chardin, Gabriel Marcel, Paul Claudel, Bernard de Clairvaux, Thérèse d'Avila, St. John of the Cross, and even some Maurice de Certeau, Emmanuel Levinas and Martin Buber, all works I had read over and over again, in the austere silence of that self-sufficient, womblike universe. I had spent there the happiest hours of my life, if 'happiness' is the word for that naked form of contentment in which the entire world is distilled into a bead of light and focused like a beam on the page before you. By contrast, after the library had become *our* place, light and focus were replaced by a derangement of the senses, as if, in its madness, the world wanted to assault and take possession of me. For someone who has never been separated from the world this may be hard to understand, but it's truly what differentiates a monk from the rest of humanity. The devotion to God is only a corollary of this separation in which he lives. Space is much more than people imagine it to be: it is *a substance* that creates its angels and demons. God would never have existed if people hadn't built churches and temples, and he himself is as much a consequence of the space of worship as this space is the result of his existence. What I mean is that the spaces we create are the outward manifestation of our psyche or imaginary world, but at the same time, they imprint themselves upon the shapes of our future creations.

"My space was under assault. It was being open to the outside world, it smelled of perfume and some other fragrances I couldn't identify, but which all spelled one word, 'woman.' This woman behaved quite differently than I had imagined women do, so it was a source of endless fascination for me to watch, and listen to her. It was as if the world in its fluidity and the myriad of shapes in it had all merged into a single, higher form of being, and this form, sitting next to me, was an open invitation to enter the world. Until then, I had never paid much attention to God's creatures—I mean, to their physical aspect. My brothers in Ligugé were rather visually unappealing—not that I'd ever thought that; it was only later that these thoughts began to enter my mind. Deformed noses, flat chins, asymmetrical jaws, greasy dark hair forming uneven patches on heads and hands, coarse hairs sprouting on ears—I noticed all this only *after* I met Alma. It was as if my eyes had suddenly opened to the world, and seeing Alma's beauty also meant being able to see the ugliness around me. And I don't mean mere ugliness of the face—this would have been nothing—but ugliness of the soul. The little flaws of my monastic brothers, of which I had been only half and vaguely aware, suddenly stood out in crisp clarity: their pettiness, their lukewarm faith, their indifference to the fate of others, of which I too had been guilty … It appeared to me that our lives weren't devoted to God, as we claimed, for had that been the case we would have been able to see Beauty; rather, we strived to eliminate everything that stirred the senses—be it beauty or ugliness—and, in so doing, to cover the world's face with a thick veil of wool in which we slept the sleep of the innocent (but not of the just). Sitting next to Alma meant having that veil torn apart, and my eyes responded by blinking, adjusting to the new light. I began to wonder whether the aura that painters put around angels' faces originates in such moments of revelation some of them must have had in the presence of a woman.

"For about two weeks I lived in Paradise—that is, thoroughly immersed in the present, without any afterthoughts. Had I had some kind of experience with women, I probably would have been tormented by the thought of our imminent separation, or by guilty dreams of repressed desires, but back then I was, as I said, a blank page. Not that I didn't desire her— but I didn't know it. What I mean is that I wasn't aware of the consequences of desire. Of course I had experienced physical desire before, but not directed toward a specific person. To have physical urges is simply a biological function, but to desire *someone* is to experience *lack*. And I was so innocent I didn't know what lack was. Not until ...

"But let me fill your glass first. Please excuse me, I didn't notice it was empty. What was I saying? Oh, yes, I was about to tell you about my fall from Paradise. It happened one glorious afternoon in the monastery garden. We had spent a lot of time together that day, and I felt drunk but thought that it must be because of the two glasses of cider I'd had at lunch. I'd walked with her under the afternoon sun, marveling at the existence of so much beauty, which I was noticing for the first time. I must have walked thousands of times under those linden trees, yet it was the first time I really took notice of the pale green of their leaves, the first time I truly saw the bushes full of rosehips, and the patches of moss stretching along the walls facing the garden. There was a fragrance in the air whose origin I couldn't determine—was it the embalmed summer air or Alma's perfume?—and a hush lifting from the grass as we stepped on it, and I was concentrating so much while listening to it that I didn't realize Alma had stopped talking and was staring at me.

"'I feel tired,' she said. 'Let's sit down.'

"We sat down on the only bench in the garden. I felt so peaceful I didn't think there was a need for words, so I closed my eyes and took a deep breath. The quiet was moving slowly through my veins when I grew increasingly aware of a slight disturbance. It felt like an animal getting closer and closer, so I opened my eyes, staring ahead. Through the corner of my left eye I saw a head almost touching mine, covered by a waterfall of dark curls. I was paralyzed. I knew this was the moment from which there was no return. I kept staring ahead. The head next to mine stopped moving too, and I could sense its tension and pulsing expectation. I knew I *was expected* to do something, but I wasn't sure what. Of course I knew what men and women do in similar situations, but this knowledge was part of a different world, a world that had nothing to do with me. I never imagined myself as an actor in such a scenario, so I just sat there, staring ahead. We must have stayed like that for minutes. Then, it occurred to me that the other head wanted me to react, so I turned my head in its direction, and in the next instant I felt something moist on my lips.

"I guess you could call that our first kiss. I was so flustered it took me a while to realize we were kissing, or rather, that *she* was kissing me. That night I spent a white night, as the French say. The sweet peace I had carried within me until then was gone. Words circled madly inside my head like swift birds, alighting now and then on bits of meaning: 'What have I done?' or 'What's going to happen now?' Twice I fell asleep for a few brief minutes only to descend into a frightening labyrinth out of which I eventually emerged covered in sweat and followed by shadows that were sending me threatening signals from the threshold I didn't dare cross. I found myself on a white beach before the open sky and, as I was about to breathe with relief, I spotted an old, wrinkled man sitting naked in the sand in all his tofu-white, flabby, revolting nudity. I moved closer to tell him to put his clothes on, but my words died on my lips: it was Brother Thomas! He turned his head to face me with a provocative smile that glowed like a slimy snake. *Has everyone gone mad?* I thought. I wanted to run away, get out of there as quickly as possible, but how? It was either the labyrinth or Brother Thomas. I was trapped. Trapped. The anxiety clutching at my breast was so strong I woke up choking. The relief to see the familiar things around me—the table with the Bible on it and the cross above, my cloak hanging on a chair—was so great I kept smiling all morning and mumbling to myself, 'All's the same, all's the same....'

"As I was lighting the candles in the church, I saw Brother Thomas, who smiled back at me, saying, 'You seem very present today. I was beginning to be worried about you. I've barely seen you for the past two weeks, and when I did, you always seemed absent.' I confirmed that, indeed, I hadn't been myself lately, but I was feeling much better today. 'As a matter of fact, I'd like to go down in the basement later and give the brothers a hand.' We had a small bookbinding workshop in the basement, but I rarely set foot in there. 'I'm sure some physical work will do you good,' said Brother Thomas, and went his way.

"For some reason, his words, in appearance so innocuous, kept reverberating in my mind. Was he trying to tell me something? Was it possible that he had taken notice of my long conversations with Alma? And if he had, and was disapproving, maybe others had noticed, too; maybe they were talking about me behind my back. They were *most certainly* talking about me behind my back. How else to explain that they'd been avoiding me during the past few days? *Were they?*

"In my sixteen years at Ligugé I'd never given a thought to what the others thought about me—or rather, I didn't think that anyone might think about me. Now, I felt that the world, which I had blissfully ignored for so long, was showing its head through the door recently cracked by Alma. After having succeeded in vanquishing the biggest sin, the sin of pride, which guides most human actions and is otherwise known as 'the ego,' my old self was coming back to me with its demands and worries about 'the others.' The realization that the peace I had attained and sustained for so many years was in jeopardy put me in a state of terrible anxiety. This may be why it took me so long to understand the feelings I had for Alma. After spending several long hours in this troubled state, I decided to see her and let her know that we could no longer see each other.

"We had made a habit of meeting in the library every afternoon after lunch, which we ate separately, I with the brothers, she with the other guests. At three o'clock I entered the library as usual, except this time with my heart pounding, and not only in my chest, but also in my throat, my belly, my temples. She was reading. I sat down in front of her, separated by the big oak table, and she acknowledged me by placing the book on the table, face down. I opened my mouth, but then I noticed her gaze shift to my right, as if she was trying to tell me something. I turned my head and saw in the right corner, behind me, one of the brothers, comfortably installed in an armchair. At first, I couldn't see his face because it was covered by the magazine he was holding, but when he turned the page, Brother Pierre's features appeared clear and unmistakable. As he did that, I watched his face: he was spying on us. He was trying to appear deep in concentration when it was clear that his eyes—one of them, at least—were following us. The anxiety in my chest was now paralleled and enhanced by another feeling I hadn't experienced in years, something I'd almost forgotten existed: anger. Images from the past, long asleep in the deep recesses of my memory, resurfaced: Brother Pierre, one year my senior, giving me a jaundiced smile when Brother Thomas introduced me to the community sixteen years earlier; Brother Pierre following me on the long halls echoing with the empty sounds of our steps; for months, Brother Pierre behind me every time I turned around. I was young then, and hadn't yet shed the raw sensitivity I'd suffered of throughout my youth, so I sensed instantly that Brother Pierre was like those male animals that, at the height of their virility, mark their territory and instinctually perceive any potential rival as an enemy. You may wonder what the rivalry was about in an environment like ours, when there was nothing we could fight over. But the sad truth is that human instincts remain even if the environment changes. At any rate, this had been sixteen years earlier, and I had learned to ignore Brother Pierre's King-of-the-Jungle syndrome, and I'd imagined that he too had learned to accept my existence. I was wrong.

"With Brother Pierre behind my back, Alma and I sat there in awkward silence, casting furtive glances at each other. Eventually, I tore a sheet of paper from a notepad lying around, and wrote in capitals, 'WE CAN NO LONGER SEE EACH OTHER.' Then, I slid the piece of paper in her direction. She lowered her eyes, taking it in, and a few seconds later I saw a transparent heart-shaped tear hanging at the edge of her nose; then another one, and another one. She was crying silently, her features unchanged by the emotional outpour—a troubling statue of sadness, its eyes the only part alive.

"I don't know when I'd last seen a woman cry. This unexpected scene threw me entirely off balance. I myself hadn't shed any tears in years, and the sight of someone crying was like witnessing a profoundly powerful event, especially since it had been caused by me. I didn't know at the time—it took the proximity of conjugal life to find out—that Alma could cry over almost anything, and two minutes later she'd be laughing again. So, I took her silent tears for a sign of muted pain, and reacted like someone confronted with a cataclysm. I began to tremble and stammer, and quickly scribbled on the sheet of paper, 'I'll go outside and wait for you.'

"A minute later she too stepped out and, forgetting about Brother Pierre, I took her by the hand and led her to the garden. It was a cloudy, chilly day, and she was lightly dressed, so she was shivering. Seeing her like that, shivering, her face wet with tears, I felt a jolt of ... How should I put it? Divine ambivalence. On the one hand, I was disturbed and wanted to wipe her tears away; on the other, she looked like a Goddess of Sorrow, and one could almost forget she was human when looking at her. Before I knew it, I was holding her in my arms and kissing her, but not like the first time. We kissed for a long time, and rain began to fall—heavy, spaced-apart drops, and then heavier, denser drops, hitting us with the gray impatience of an autumn afternoon, though it was still August. Thunder shook the skies and made us run toward the building, and as we stepped inside, soaked and holding hands, I saw Brother Pierre's face in the window. For a brief instant our eyes met—his were colder than the rain.

"That night I experienced *lack, deep lack,* for the first time since I'd entered the monastery. I tossed and turned, replaying in my head the scene in the garden, feeling that she naturally belonged in my arms, and that without her my arms were robbed of something essential. For the next several days, Alma and I met whenever I could steal away from my obligations, now in the garden, now in the library, now behind a pillar in the cloister, now in some dark nook behind the stairs. I began to understand why they use the word 'intoxicated' to describe such states—for I was intoxicated. Even my usual caution had almost deserted me, in spite of the fact that Alma kept saying that she always felt a gaze piercing her back and had the unmistakable feeling that someone was watching us. Indeed, one evening, as I was telling her good-night, my eyes caught the trembling edge of a gray cloak hiding behind a pillar.

"'Who's there?' I asked in a loud, angry voice.

"The gray cloak stepped out, and Brother Pierre's silhouette emerged in the dim yellow light.

"'It's me, only me,' he said, with an arrogant smile.

"I let the arm with which I'd been holding Alma fall, and watched him watch us in silence.

"'So I see,' I said.

"The next morning after *laudes*, Brother Thomas accosted me and summoned me to his office. He did this without looking me in the eye, so I knew what to expect. When I entered his office, the first thing I saw was a black robe at the top of which Father Paul's rosy cheeks welcomed me. Brother Thomas stood behind his desk with his hands united as in prayer, and both he and Father Paul appeared very solemn. I wasn't invited to sit down, so I just stood there, waiting.

"'I assume you know why you are here,' Brother Thomas said, this time looking me straight in the eye.

"'I'll know if you tell me.'

"Where was this desire to defy coming from? It was as if a voice I didn't know I had inside me was all of a sudden making itself heard.

"'Very well, then. We've heard certain rumors that are incompatible with your calling.'

"I couldn't not take advantage of the slight lapse in logic of his sentence, so I answered:

"'If the rumors are incompatible with my calling, then why do you pay them any heed?'

"'It is up to you to behave in a way that doesn't invite any rumors,' said Brother Thomas with the harshest tone I'd heard him use in the sixteen years I'd known him.

"And then, all my barely contained countenance, the humility and reserve I thought were now as much a part of me as my limbs, were shed like an old skin, uncovering the defiant youth I once was.

"'If you have anything to say about my behavior, then spell it out!'

"Brother Thomas's face dropped, leaving him with his mouth agape, as if he wasn't sure he'd heard well. Then, after a few seconds of perplexed silence, Father Paul spoke:

"'I thought you might want to confess. It would do you good.'

"'I'll let you know when I'm ready for confession, Father,' the same rebellious youth said, speaking through my possessed mouth and watching me from afar.

* * *

"A few hours later, Alma told me that her departure date was in two days. It took me some time to understand that this was the date set long in advance, and it had nothing to do with the downward spiral I'd been caught in. All my life seemed to be sliding downward, and it was happening so quickly I could only watch, helpless. I didn't know what the future had in store for me, but I knew I couldn't go back. And so, I was forced to do something I'd never done before: think about the future. You have to understand that living in a monastery is like living on an island of arrested time. The future doesn't exist there. Everything happens in the present, following the bells' tolls, which slice each day into equal portions eaten away by Time's industrious ants. Now, for the first time I had to look into the future. Of this nebulous future I only knew one thing: it couldn't be without Alma. And then, it dawned on me that Alma wasn't any freer than I was. I remembered she'd mentioned when we first met something about a husband—but that was an eternity ago. In two days she had to go back to this man whose existence I had totally ignored, but who was as real as I was.

"That night I dared to imagine for the first time my life with Alma. We were living in a small cottage in the French countryside with a pear tree in the courtyard, which in the early fall put out big, golden fruit and cast a large shadow on the pebbled earth at which a few stray chickens picked, bored and idle, while a gray cat with white paws stretched on the nearby wooden fence. Alma lay in a hammock reading, and I was about to go to church for the vespers service. I was still a monk. Yes, even in my most secret world, I was still wearing the monastic cloak. For, if I took off that cloak, what else could I do? Who would hire me? To do what? The only thing I was good at, apart from praying, was building small pieces of wooden furniture— you know, the kind of things a carpenter without much training could do. Maybe I could be a carpenter! And tossing and turning, I began to distinguish through a dense fog of tangled, unfinished thoughts, the outline of our living room with the shelves I would build for our books, a round walnut table in the dining area, and a large oak bed in our bedroom. And, as I opened the bedroom door I saw a woman in a long, white silk gown reclining on the bed with a cascade of dark curls circling her face and running down her spine. The woman lifted her head and, when our eyes met, I woke up.

"I woke up with the same lack inside me as the previous night, as if my body had been hollowed out the way a vegetable is when a cook prepares it to later fill it with stuffing. The image of a hollowed tomato flashed before my eyes, and then that of an egg with mayonnaise, something my mother used to cook and which I had loved as a child, and the image of my mother cooking and of me as a boy made me think of the States, and thus, little by little, I came to wonder whether, after all, I might someday return to the States and live there with Alma an unassuming, happy life in a small, quaint town on the East or West Coast.

"As scenes from my future life were playing before my sleepy eyes, I heard the bell ring, and I jumped out of bed, but still, I arrived too late. Joining the singing brothers, I noticed a frown on Brother Thomas's face. You may not know this, but the choir of the Ligugé Abbey is one of the best in France. It is, in fact, what I miss most when I think of those days past. I still believe that nothing can compare with those pure notes soaring to the sky—not like a plot advancing toward its climax or like a hunter nearing its prey, but rather, staying at the same level, as if the sky were not above us but was already only a memory filtered through our chant, a remembrance intoned over and over, in repetitive, autistic circles. Yes, I miss that repetitive, monotonous drone that impregnated life there and made it so peaceful. Ever since leaving the monastery I've strived to order my life in accordance with that rhythm, to strike the same long, monotonous cord as a Gregorian chant. Do you know what disharmonic music was called in the Renaissance? The 'devil's music'—and it was banned, by the way. Likewise, for a monk, to live a life in a disharmonious way is to walk in the devil's way.

"Well, you know the ending of my story: Alma returned to her husband, and eventually they divorced. I suppose there is no point in my going on."

"Did you meet him? Her first husband, I mean."

"Sure I did, eventually. An unsavory character. Resentful and vengeful. At first, he didn't want to grant her the divorce.

And after, he kept finding ways of interfering in our life. It took him almost a year after Alma and I got married to stop harassing her. In the end, he found another woman, and he and Alma made peace. This was shortly before my mother died. My mother's death was a very trying time for me ... I began to remember things I'd thought long forgotten, hidden in some locked chambers of my brain, which a magic key had suddenly let loose. I even remembered—all of a sudden—names of first-grade classmates, kids who had come once or twice by our house, who had entirely disappeared from my memory, and now surged out of the dark, wanting to be acknowledged. It was as if her death had triggered a strange mnemonic device, a whole past life demanding to be revisited before succumbing to final oblivion. And so, caught in this tangle of recollections, on top of the pain caused by her death, I was incapable of thinking straight. I couldn't deal with the funeral arrangements, and my sister, Patrice, was in France. That's why when Alma offered to take care of it I didn't say no. You must know that at the time, No. 1, as she calls him, owned a funeral parlor. Alma told me that she would make arrangements with him, and, although I wasn't thrilled about it, I gave my approval. After all, aren't all funeral homes more or less the same? What was there to fear? Now, before I go any further, tell me, have you heard this story before?"

"Sort of."

"You 'sort of' heard it from whom?"

"Some snippets from Alma and some from No. 1."

"I see.... Well then, I'm not going to bore you with all the details, though I'd be curious to know what he had to say for himself. Even now, after all this time, my stomach tightens at the thought.... What would you do if the man in charge of your mother's funeral insulted your guests by giving them obscene fortune cookies? If the man in charge of your mother's funeral found it appropriate to exhibit for the occasion sexual paraphernalia and to transform her body into some kind of fatal vamp? Clearly, this was his revenge, though I hadn't done anything to him. I didn't steal Alma from him, as he thinks. I couldn't steal her because he had already lost her. But if his plan was to get revenge, it certainly worked because he managed to taint my mother's memory forever. Curiously, although the Architect was the one who wronged me, I was never as angry with him as I was with that first husband of hers. It may be because in some way I felt guilty of a great offense, and losing Alma was a just punishment."

"What do you mean by 'a great offense'?"

"Oh, it was not the fact that I left the monastery, no … It was something entirely different. But it's a long story, are you sure you want to hear it?"

He nodded: yes. And so I told him the story.

After my mother's death I'd inherited some money and the small house in which she'd lived in Boston. My sister was still living in France, so she wasn't interested in it, while Alma and I needed a place to live after she finished her Masters, so we decided that it was the right moment for us to have our own house. By that time I had started to work as a carpenter and gained confidence in my skills, so we moved to Boston and were about to move into the house when, as chance would have it, I happened upon an architecture show at the Museum of Fine Arts. It was a late autumn day, and I was walking sluggishly on Huntington Avenue toward our hotel in a rather melancholy mood, carrying a bag of groceries and tugging at my woolen coat collar to protect my throat against the razor-sharp wind, and, as I passed by the museum, I raised my eyes and saw the sign "American Houses." I remember thinking that this was the perfect opportunity to get some ideas for our house, though why I thought that I don't know, since all I wanted at the time was for us to move into the house as quickly as possible.

It was a show of photographs from the 1950s to the present, with various styles of houses from all over the country. As I walked around, alone with my brown bag amid all those black-and-white images, I began to feel like a character in a black-and-white movie who suddenly awakes in a world full of color and hope. There were no colors on the walls, but the multitude of possibilities taking shape before me was so dizzying that my head hurt. Squinting my eyes to read the labels under the dim, stingy light, I was becoming acquainted with such terms as colonial revival, Tudor style, Italianate style, and others, less exotic, which I'd known as a teenager but had forgotten during the years spent in France. I think my favorite styles of the exhibit were Tudor and the bungalows and cottages, in particular the A-framed wooden houses. The latter were small cottages of dark wood built in an A-shape with one and a half floors, the upper one displaying a dormer-style window. They looked like fairytale houses, but without the Victorian decorations and superfluous curves and curlicues. They had a rustic simplicity I found calming and peaceful. Standing before one such picture, I began to add other elements to it: a white sheep sleeping like a big ball of cotton candy on the expanse of grass in front of the house, with a young woman kneeling next to it and petting it gently. I was so satisfied with this mental image that I took a notebook out of my pocket and drew some lines, but the result was rather pathetic, so, sighing and smiling, I put the notebook back and continued my visit.

A similar simplicity was also present in the craftsman houses, I thought. Yes, in the end, the style that was the most congenial and appropriate to my nature was craftsman. I pictured myself and Alma in one of those high-beamed ceiling wooden houses with a front wood deck and a tall brick chimney from which the smoke curled up against a crisp, blue sky. I had never owned a house and never felt the need until now. There was something so tenderly tranquil in those black-and-white photographs—so many domestic universes enclosed within those rectangular walls of wood, or stone, or brick, with those solid or multipaned windows, and front doors framed by straight or carved, ornate wood in dark trims contrasting with the pale colors of the houses. I would have liked to inhabit a hundred bodies and linger in each of those places, a week in a body and a house. But every single body and every single house had only one woman: Alma. In the end, it was for her that I wanted a house, and not just any house, a house that would be a symbol of our love. The more I thought about it, the more excited and energized I became, like a man who had just awakened from a long sleep with a clear vision of what his life's purpose would be from then on. It seemed as if everything I'd been and done in life till then was just a preparation for this moment, and all fell into place now: the house and the inheritance, my walking on this street and the chance discovery of this show.

I must have spent at least three hours staring at those photographs and daydreaming. I went back to the hotel almost running, and before I even put the groceries in our little fridge, I blurted out my discovery. I was still dazed by that black-and-white procession of imagined paradises, and wanted Alma to share in my dream, to see that it was touchable and doable, that it was, as they say, meant to be. But Alma reacted with far less enthusiasm than I expected; in fact, she began to ask me questions that challenged my whole project, making me feel guilty that I had even thought about it.

"So, you are saying that instead of simply moving into a perfectly good house and saving your mother's money for the future, considering that I still don't have a full-time job and you don't have a clientele in this city yet, you are saying that instead, we should go ahead and spend all that money, possibly even more, in order to build something we don't really need."

Her logic paralyzed me. All along I'd had in my head the image of an earthly Paradise, which was going to be my gift to her, and now she was telling me she "didn't really need it." "And besides," she continued in the same querulous tone, "where are we going to live while the construction is going on?"

"We could rent something," I said, my own enthusiasm considerably dampened.

"Rent? And how are we going to pay the rent, if I may ask?" She sounded angry, as if I had offended her in some way.

"What do you mean, 'How are we going to pay the rent'? The way we've done it so far. I'll work."

"The way *we*'ve done it so far? I may have forgotten something, but as far as I remember, so far *I* have been the one working."

I had felt very guilty while she worked as a teaching assistant and I was still adapting to my new life and my birth country, but she'd always reassured me. Now, for the first time, the truth was in the open. I clenched my teeth, bit my tongue, and went to bed. I was so distressed I felt nauseous all night. You must have experienced at least once how, after having run to someone with what you thought was a glorious gift or piece of news, you have to watch, in dismay, how your gift is made into a joke, and you are so embarrassed by its being trampled down and crushed before your very eyes that you can't even pick it up to dust it off and put back in your pocket what's left of it.

We made peace in the morning, and I could tell she regretted her words. But you know how words are; they don't die easily. We moved into my mother's house soon after, and for

several weeks I was busy repairing cabinets, doors, and what-
not, and replacing door knobs, bulbs, and sink fixtures. Alma
found a job as a substitute teacher in the neighborhood, and
Christmas was, as they say, in the air. I bought a tree a few days
before Christmas and, as I took it down from the car roof and
held it, trying to regain my breath before dragging it through the
rapidly growing snow, I felt a surge of happiness inside me, and
I stood there holding the tree to better enjoy that feeling. I could
feel the compact snow under my feet, and the crisp silence,
which absorbed my hushed breath under the bell-jar sky. It was
getting dark, and scattered snowflakes could be seen here and
there through the milky light coming from our house. Through
one of the lit windows I could make out a woman's silhouette
moving back and forth, attending to something, very likely a pot
on the stove. The sensation of the cold snowflakes melting on
my cheeks and the imagined warmth in that kitchen with the
woman busily moving about gave my blood a sudden rush. I felt
like laughing and crying all at once. The house looked a bit eerie
in the night, with its eclectic styles and additions as a result of
having gone through two owners, my mother being the second.
The lower half was made of local, dark gray granite, while the
upper half was cedar shingles, a melancholy bluish hue, which
at twilight bled into the ashen horizon. After the death of my
father, some crook (whom she called "a close friend") convinced
my mother to make an addition to rent it out, and an addition
she made. She converted the shingled roof into a loft—I think
the style is called mansarded; maybe she chose it as an homage
to her French origin, maybe because she was confused by the
name, since in French a "*mansarde*" is equivalent to a loft. At any
rate, the loft had the sloped sides and the roof specific to the
mansard style, and a tiny dormer through which the light fell like
a golden sheaf thrown onto the sea-blue bed quilt. Following

the advice of the same well-meaning friend, she painted the loft a bright lilac, but luckily, the color has faded over time, and now it's almost the same shade as the rest of the house.

Yes, the house stood there like an awkward but charming teenager in mismatched garments, and now that I could identify its various styles, I no longer had the ambivalent feelings I'd previously nourished for it; rather, as I contemplated it, I experienced the tenderness a parent might feel at the sight of his handicapped child.

"Poor house," I said, stretching my arm toward it, as if to caress its tousled hair. The house sighed and blinked in response. Blinked? Yes, the light in the kitchen went off, and the one in the living room was switched on, as the woman moved from one room into the other. My hair was wet with radiant, teary snowflakes, and my feet were cold. I took the tree and opened the door.

The next evening, the living room of the French mansarded house was well lit, and I was decorating the tree with Alma's help. We never had Christmas trees back at the monastery. Whenever I tell people this they are surprised, but why should they be? After all, there is nothing more pagan than celebrating a tree. I remember having read as a child tales about trees planted on the spot where a young man or woman had been buried. Well, this is what a green tree is: a symbol of a life cut short. But a tree with red bows, and sparkling silver and golden foil in it? That's like a savage painting his chest and getting ready to go to war. The first winter Alma had proposed to get a Christmas tree I refused categorically; the following year she showed up with a small potted tree with a red bow at the top, so this year I went and bought the tree myself. If we were going to have a Christmas tree, at least it should look like a real tree. It was a tall, beautiful, and strongly scented fir tree, and decorating it brought back long-forgotten memories from my childhood. This may be, in fact, the definition of happiness: reliving your best childhood moments. Being a child again. As we hung red and yellow round ornaments and silver stars with sugary coated surfaces on our tall, green tree, I was a happy, innocent child, and my wife's and my mother's images melted into each other, steeped in that eternal, sepia glow of old memories.

After we finished, and we sat down on the little woolen rug in front of the fireplace, watching the flames flicker, some retreating into nothingness, as others took over in an explosion of orange and red—there is nothing as fascinating as watching a fire, maybe only listening to the rain—I thought that at that moment I had everything. There was nothing else in the world I needed or wanted. We sat like that for a while, letting our faces and hands absorb the heat and the fire's shadows, and then Alma got up and went to fetch something. She returned with a large hardcover, a black-and-white coffee-table book, which she handed to me, smiling. *Boston Houses*, read the one-inch letters on the front cover.

"I got it at the museum. It has some of the pictures in that exhibit. I wanted to give it to you for Christmas, but maybe we can celebrate earlier."

I was, of course, touched. So touched that I didn't even open it, but put it next to us on the floor, like a relic, and spent the entire evening holding the giver in my arms. But the next day, as I was resting on the couch in front of the fireplace, I picked up the book from the floor and absentmindedly began to turn its pages. At first, I looked at those houses without really seeing them, content to lie there next to our Christmas tree while snowflakes big as dandelion puffs drifted beyond the windowpanes. Then, my eyes began to distinguish the outlines of a house I'd particularly liked at the exhibit, little by little bringing it into focus, and, as I did that, I found myself imagining a different life, in a different house, like the one in the picture, the way I used to do in my early twenties before I moved to France. Back then I used to go to all the open houses in the neighborhood, and all the house sales I could get to in the immediate vicinity. It was like a secret vice I had, seeing all those incarnations of possible lives, imagining all the people I could be and places I could live in. Every weekend I'd spend hours in those places, sniffing around like some rich heir interested in making a valuable purchase, when in fact all I wanted were textures, smells, angles, and curves. Then I'd come home and lie in bed for hours with my hands crossed over my chest, and daydream about what I'd seen. I just couldn't live within the boundaries of my own body, within the four walls of a single life. That's why, when I discovered French cathedrals and monasteries, I felt as if I was finally coming *home*. Yes, I know, most people would wonder how someone for whom a body and a normal home aren't enough can be content living in a monastery. For them, living in a monastery is synonymous with giving up something. They don't think of it as an experience that redefines space and time. If there is something sacred about the space of a monastery it is because it can absorb one's restlessness, distill it, and make it soar like a song all the way to the gates of heaven.

But to come back to the day when I was lying on the couch holding the book of Boston houses near my chest. My eyes moved lazily from horizontal to vertical lines until they finally settled on what seemed like a living room. It was an unusual space in that it wasn't rectangular. One of its sides was curved, egg-like, with two soft angles at both ends, and all along the curved line, large, multipaned windows were cut into the wall, leaving only a little bit of space for the white stucco near both ends. On top of that, the white beamed ceiling was slanted, lower at the far end and higher at the other. As I looked at that strange structure, the surge of energy I'd felt when visiting the exhibit came back, as if I were discovering that there was a new dimension out there, and it was up to me to enter it. I later understood—later, when we had begun remodeling the new house—that remodeling one's space is entering a new dimension, and that we are just as much made by the path crossed by our feet, as our feet are made by the earthen ribbon under them. But it's not these abstract thoughts that crossed my mind at the time; no, my thoughts turned immediately to what the implications of that unusually curved space were for me and Alma. If one could build such a house and twist space in such unexpected configurations, if a house could have such openness, giving itself to light with all its windowpanes and absorbing it like a seed ready to sprout, that meant that one could also build a house that would embody a secret dream, a house whose walls would sing a hymn to Love. And my desire, which I thought had left me, of building this house and of living in it with Alma until the end of our days, grew again, and this time I knew I couldn't let it go because it was linked to my need for molding the space in keeping with my own monastic rhythm.

And so, I began to look for inspiration not only in the book on Boston houses, but every time I was out. I found myself staring at strangers' houses and stopping in front of them, stealing a certain architectural element I thought appealing, and adding it to *our* house. Sometimes, when I really liked a place, I had to restrain myself from knocking at the door and asking the occupants to let me in to study the way the entry hall was linked to the living room, or admire the vaulted openings that replaced the doors, or touch the walls and inquire about the intriguing construction materials. Suspicious eyes followed my movements from behind drawn curtains, and I felt like a voyeur feeding his shameful passion. I felt even guiltier in Alma's presence, having to pretend that I too had settled into our domestic routine, and that the space we inhabited was where I expected to live from then on. When I finally confessed, I was forced to do so because of an unforeseen circumstance. My sister, Patrice, who had recently moved to the States from France and was visiting us, mentioned one night at dinner— with uncharacteristic enthusiasm, an enthusiasm verging, in fact, on schoolgirl giddiness—the "extraordinary man" (*"vraiment, un homme extraordinaire"*), an architect she'd met the previous night at some friends of hers. The architect was from San Francisco, but had been living in Boston for the past year, working on a big public project.

"Imagine," she said, "a slightly leaner and taller Luciano Pavarotti quoting nonchalantly Angelus Silesius, Rabelais, and Basho as he wolfs down two huge steaks, one of which was supposed to be for a guest who had had the good sense not to show up, and then offering to help me with the half steak left on my plate. 'I don't like waste,' he said. 'I was raised to finish everything on my plate. My grandmother always thought I was too skinny. She's from Sicily, you know.... I guess I have to thank her for this.' And he vigorously patted his paunch, as if he was about to throw it, like an oversize ball, across the field."

"Well, that's an interesting coincidence," I said, trying to find something to stare at on my plate, and thus avoid looking at Alma.

"Why is that?"

"Because I might need an architect. I've been thinking about possibly remodeling this house." I said this while staring at my plate, whose ostentatious, flowery design I was noticing for the first time. It had belonged, like many of the things we now owned, to my mother.

And I began to tell her about the exhibit I'd seen and the many possibilities we had to transform this place from a cut-and-paste abode to a true, harmonious Dwelling. Throughout my long explanation I didn't dare look at Alma, who had gotten up and was cleaning the table without a word. And we never did talk about it, neither that night nor after. We simply moved on to the next stage, although in hindsight it's clear that from then on we were simply pawns in a predetermined game, and that my arrogant desire made me lose her.

Before moving into my mother's house we barely had a roof over our heads. We only owned enough things to live day by day, and I never thought we needed more. But after we had more than we actually needed, I grew restless and drunk with the desire to have more, not more things or money, but the desire to turn the excess we already possessed into a space that would show the world and the gods how happy we were. I didn't know at the time that happiness is something one should hide and protect from other eyes like a stolen good—for it is stolen, or rather, it is lent to us with a big interest rate. That's why I can't be angry with the Architect. On the contrary, I feel a certain solidarity with him, now that he's going through what I've been through. But no, I don't feel "vindicated" at all. I sometimes pause to wonder at the unpredictable turns our life takes, and how, when I first met the Architect, I never would have dreamt he would one day take my place. Even when he started to visit us regularly, often without a specific reason, I didn't suspect anything. You see, I never thought Alma would leave me. I had received her presence in my life as a gift, and gifts aren't usually taken back from you unless you are punished.

The day after my sister gave me the Architect's phone number, I picked up the phone and called him. We agreed on a day to meet, and for some reason, I thought I should let my sister know. A few days later, as I was lazily looking through the dining room window, I saw a stranger in our courtyard, a portly man dressed in a well-cut woolen coat, who, with intent and precise gestures, was busying himself cutting off dried branches from our oak tree. He then shook the debris off his leather gloves and advanced toward our front door. When I opened the door, before he even answered my greeting, he gestured toward the tree and spoke, as if continuing a conversation:

"That guy over there is in need of a good trim."

Then he directed toward me a large, warm smile, and, taking his gloves off, shook not one but both my hands with both of his hands. I led him through the house, telling him about my intentions, and he listened with a detached air, stopping now and then before a painting or the embarrassingly ornate fireplace framed by paneled walls, and whose marble top he stroked with his right hand, while he kept his left one in his pocket and his head turned around, as if on a spring, head and hands focused on completely different things until, after having toured the house, they finally came together into a unified, unidirectional body. Then, straightening his body under the black-bearded head, he used his right hand to adjust his glasses and, with a light swing of the body, turned his eyes in my direction. For the first time since entering the house he was looking *at* me. He had a piercing, severe gaze, like a teacher in a bad mood who had found a student on whom his moodiness could alight. I let him stare at me—after all, he was my guest—and who knows how long he would have done it if the bell hadn't rung.

I wasn't expecting anyone. I opened, and whom should I see but Patrice holding a big package wrapped in white paper. With uncharacteristic jovialness she stepped in before I could even invite her. She took off her coat with a dramatic swing of the hips, hung it up by the door, and advanced toward us still carrying that unending smile on her face. For the next hour I observed her perform a birdlike dance around the Architect, as the latter kept straightening his glasses with the same detached expression.

"What's in the package?" I asked.

She unwrapped it with the swift gesture of a magician pulling a rabbit out of a hat, revealing four enormous slices of cheesecake topped with raspberry sauce. The Architect's face underwent an immediate transformation, the way a grandfather's face might at the sight of his toddler grandson. Patrice went into the kitchen to fetch plates and silverware, and we sat down on the small living room couch, my left knee touching the Architect's right one. When Patrice returned with three plates, one of which sported two slices of cake, her smile was still there, except this time it had the awkward crookedness of a person tired of having to stand for too long on one foot. I was embarrassed for her; the Architect, on the other hand, seemed perfectly at ease.

"Ah, cheesecake," he said, grabbing the plate with two slices and making a visible dent in one of them, but not before carefully spreading the raspberry sauce evenly onto the cake's top.

"There is an inherent beauty in the fruit topping that decorates a cake," he declared, his mouth full, "and not simply because of the contrast in color between the fruit and the cake. Do you know why that is?"

We were, of course, silent, and he continued:

"It's because of the basic law that underlies anything beautiful, which is that beauty is by essence *excessive*; that is, it transcends usefulness. If you put something *on top* of something else, it becomes naturally excessive, and therefore beautiful."

Patrice took a pensive breath. "Hmm," she said. "Would you say that that is always true?"

"Of course not," he replied, laughing. "Just look at me on top of this couch!"

And he laughed so hard his belly seemed to become a separate organism, jumping in disharmonious bursts, as if to prove his point.

I hadn't touched my cake, so, after he gobbled both of his, I offered him mine. To my surprise, he accepted with a disconcerting matter-of-factness. As he ate the third slice, Patrice said with forced nonchalance:

"You know, you were right the other night. It's Angelus Silesius, not Shakespeare, who said, 'A rose is without why. It blooms because it blooms.'"

"Of course I was right. You mixed up your roses." And he laughed again, his mouth still full. When he finished, he stood up and took his plate and fork to the kitchen, followed by Patrice, who kept asking him to let her do it. I heard their voices mingle and argue over the kitchen sink, him saying, "But I like doing it; it's no trouble at all," and her fighting—presumably—to stop him, as the water ran and covered with its sound their improvised theater. By the time they came out of the kitchen they could have washed a whole stack of dishes. Immediately, the Architect excused himself, saying he had another appointment, and we agreed to meet another time.

The next time I saw him it was without Patrice's knowledge. Alma was at home, too. It was a rainy day in mid-February, and he entered the house like Poseidon ascending from the sea, dripping water all over the wooden floors from his oversized umbrella and colossal body. To think of it, my most vivid memories of him depict him in the midst of the elements: a downpour, a snowstorm, a blooming garden with him lecturing Alma and the trees, his dark head circled by the sun's radiant halo. He was—still is, I presume—the kind of man who "makes an impression." When he entered a room, he took in the view, and, simultaneously, the view took him in. A man can have all kinds of gifts, but his was most unusual: he changed the space he entered. The rest of us, when entering a room, modify our behavior and posture according to the environment; in his case, it was the opposite: his surroundings were molded and remade in order to adjust to his being there.

Later, I thought dozens of times about this day, the way we think after an accident: how different our life would have been had we taken the road to the left, rather than the one to the right, or had we gotten into the car five minutes later, or taken the bus that day.... I played each scene over and over in my mind, wondering at what point exactly the two of them understood what was happening. At what insignificant moment of our conversation did their eyes meet with the knowledge of what was about to happen?

Once, I came home earlier than expected, and there was no one in the house. For no precise reason I went to open the back door, and was surprised to find the two of them on the bench behind the house. They weren't *doing* anything, but there was something peculiar about their stillness and the very quality of the air surrounding them. They were shadowed by our tall maple tree, whose clearly outlined leaves left a soft echo of green light against the sky's pale nudity. They seemed like characters in a painting, hieratic and elusive. I watched them for a few seconds before I announced my presence, fascinated by what I was seeing. And even then, *I didn't see.* They reacted with unease when I greeted them, and that seemed odd, but I didn't delve into it. I've always believed that to attempt to penetrate everything, to unveil every single secret around us, is akin to blasphemy, and that if we do so we'll pay for it sooner or later. Sacredness is merely another name for strangeness, and our ability to receive it is inversely proportional to our desire to uncover the reason of things.

That was the first time I saw them alone in our garden. From then on, the Architect became a regular presence in our home, having dinner with us or dropping by in the afternoon. As I worked on some project in our front courtyard, chiseling wood and making it into chairs and nightstands, every now and then I would catch a glimpse of them. They were usually in the back garden, though sometimes they took strolls around the house, discussing this and that animatedly —books, art, music.

You may think of me, "What an idiot! He deserved to lose her!" But, truly, I found nothing wrong with him being there. At least, not in the beginning. But I did notice a change in Alma, who had become dreamier, lost in thought for hours. After a few months, her absentmindedness turned into downright hostility. When we reached that point, I knew that something had happened; and yet, even then I refused to confront her or to ask for an explanation. The more hostile she was, the more I retreated into my shell: my work, my music, my prayers. But the sacred place where I came each time after we had a disagreement was the Love Tower, which was almost done.

I had imagined our Love Tower emerging in the middle of our living room and shooting straight up to our bedroom on the third floor where one could climb by way of a spiral staircase. But the Architect convinced me that it was much better to build the tower outside, against the house's front wall, preferably in an asymmetrical way, following one of H. H. Richardson's designs with the tower built on the left side within the angle made by the main gable. That meant that the tower would cut into the front wall itself, which had to be partially torn down, but still, it was less messy and distracting than building it right in the middle of the house.

There is something about coiled stairs that makes one think of a hard-to-reach, awe-inspiring sanctuary. Anyone who has climbed the stairs of the Tower of Pisa, or some old basilica in the French countryside, has had this feeling of moving upward toward a precious, invisible gift. You climb in the dark, brushing against the tight walls, your mind focused on a point you can't see, and then, all of a sudden, you are up there, and the sky opens up, a triumphant downpour of blinding light. You sit down at the top of the stairs, breathing heavily, full of inner brightness.

It was that brightness that I wanted to bring to our home, and the sensation of reaching it after a symbolic trial. And also the feminine flow of the spiral, the mystery of its coiled breathing. But, as it turned out, we couldn't fit a double bed through the tower's narrow stairs; we were barely able to take two twin mattresses up there. So, we ended up sleeping in twin beds, or rather, mattresses, laid directly on the floor. Yes, this was the prosaic result of my dream of a Love Tower. And each time my wife came up to bed, she used the opportunity to remind me of my failure:

"Two years of living in a house torn apart, of having to put up with construction workers strolling inside my house as on Main Street. And for what? To sleep on the floor."

Her words brought tears to my eyes, mainly because she was right, but also because she never mentioned that, in spite of everything, we did have the Tower. In fact, I had the feeling— and it was a frightening sensation—that she resented the Tower and what it represented.

The night we celebrated its construction I put votive candles on both sides of each step all the way up to our bedroom, and built a fire in the fireplace, although it was a mild, late spring night. We had the Architect over for dinner, our only guest. Alma was in a bad mood, having almost stepped on one of the candles and burnt herself.

"I did suggest red roses instead of candles," the Architect said, his mouth still full of the mashed potatoes and steak Alma had prepared—the steak, as always, overcooked. When Alma had said at the beginning of the meal, smiling apologetically, "I think I might have overcooked the steak again," the Architect had smiled back and, pouring his second glass of Pinot Noir, answered that it was all for the best, since we now had an extra reason to drink more wine.

"Yes, I should have listened to you," I answered promptly, with an involuntary, masochistic reflex. After this, no one said anything else, and an uncomfortable silence grew between us. Not another word was spoken for the rest of the dinner, and all you could hear was the sound of the silverware punctuated by an occasional "hmm" or a dry cough. When we finished, we each took a seat away from each other—Alma on the couch, the Architect in the only armchair, and I on a chair—holding our wine glasses and listening intently to the crackling in the fireplace. It was the kind of silence and setting perfect for a couple, but we were three, and this changed everything. For the first time I sensed—and this, with a shiver throughout my entire body—that the Architect's presence in our home was *monstrous*, an act against nature, a perversion of a couple's intimacy. This feeling was so palpable that it was impossible for the two of them to be unaware of it, and yet the Architect gave no sign that he intended to leave. We all kept staring at the fire, with the silence like a taut bow between us. Eventually, when the silence became unbearable, I got up and said:

"Well, I am rather tired. I think I'll go to bed."

I expected, of course, that Alma would join me, and the Architect would have no choice but to leave. But, after shifting slightly on the couch and moving her hair from one shoulder to the other, she continued to stare into the fire without a word. So I stood there for a few, long seconds, uncertain and stupefied. I couldn't say that I changed my mind and didn't want to go to bed any longer; but I couldn't leave the two of them in my living room at almost midnight, either.

"So," I said, stupidly, scanning their faces and hoping for a miracle—but there was no miracle. "I guess I'll go then," I continued, but didn't move.

At that moment, the Architect raised his face and, looking me in the eye, said, "Good-night then." "Good-night," I answered mechanically. For a second, we looked at each other, and I saw pity in his eyes, and then I had to leave, because I could no longer contain my tears.

And this is when I finally understood that our marriage was over. After that, Alma no longer came to our bedroom. And the irony was complete: our love ended the very day we celebrated the completion of the Love Tower. Later, when the process of our separation began, Alma called our tower "a mausoleum" and "a museum." As for myself, I knew I was being punished in the same way those who wished to reach the sky with a Tower had once been punished by having their desire turned on its head and transformed into a Tower of Discord. The Love Tower was my Babel, and I was the architect of my own destruction. The fact that Alma left me for an architect was proof of this. That's why I never blamed her. That's why I don't complain. That's why, when all is said and done, the Architect himself was no more than an instrument in a design preceding his own.

№ 3

I could tell he didn't believe me, but it was the truth: I had no idea where she was. Or, to be more exact: I didn't know where she was, but I suspected she might be hiding in a Japanese temple.

"*Which* temple?" he asked.

"This, I couldn't say. It could be one of the places we've stayed at, or, on the contrary, she might have chosen a place I am not familiar with. I guess you could try to contact the temples we've stayed at. Have you ever been lodged in a temple? Actually, you don't really stay in the temple itself, but in an adjacent guest house, a sort of inn called a *shukubo*.

"The first time we stayed in a temple lodging was a few months after she moved in with me, two years before the Olympic Games in Nagano. The Japanese were looking for Western architects for their Olympic village, and I got hired for a project. I was there for several weeks, and Alma came to visit. And you know Alma.... When she discovered Zenko-ji, a Shinto temple from the seventeenth century, she spent all her time loitering around it. During the two weeks she was in Nagano she went to that damn temple every day, each time coming back loaded with a fresh dose of excitement, like a housewife returning from the market with a bag full of groceries. Going on and on about the monks' clothes and their wooden shoes, and how the head monk slapped her over the head with his prayer beads as he gave his blessing to the kneeling faithful, and how that was a sign—a sign of *what*? People with empty lives and empty heads are always looking for signs that would give a meaning to their vacuum."

"Excuse me, but you shouldn't say such things about her," he said, displaying the didacticism of an ethics professor. "After all, she was your wife."

"Why not? What meaning can there be in the fact that some Japanese man dressed in a funny-looking robe, who spends his mornings chanting *a, o, u, e* in various tones, hits you over the head with some beads? What meaning except that he has no manners? The search for meaning ... Any idiot educated by Oprah searches for meaning these days."

"Alma never watches Oprah," he hastened to point out.

"Yes, yes, I know. And, by the way, when I say 'any idiot' I don't mean Alma. An idiot she's not. Or rather, she isn't just 'any idiot,' she's a very special kind of idiot. The sophisticated kind."

"I would like to point out that when you insult my fiancée you insult me," he declared with the same earnest tone.

God, I thought. *This poor fellow has no sense of humor. He couldn't last more than a week with Alma.*

"Hmm ..." I cleared my vocal cords. "I could also point out that having a wife—even an ex-wife—entitles you to more than having a fiancée does. But I'd rather go back to our story. Zenko-ji."

I explained that many Japanese temples, Zenko-ji included, have *shukubos* within their precincts, that is, lodgings for tourists whose hosts may be monks or lay people who live there with their families. The second time I had to travel to Nagano, Alma and I chose to stay in a *shukubo*, because we were given breakfast and dinner. Breakfast, I could have done without—who wants to eat rice, Miso soup, marinated plum, and some black, wormlike little creatures for breakfast? But dinner was worth it. Not for the taste—those strange flavors aren't made for our Western palate—but for the pleasure of looking at it. The sight of a Japanese red-lacquered platter full with dishes of the most varied colors and textures makes you understand that we Westerners are a primitive civilization. I am not using the word "primitive" in the anthropological sense, but rather as a synonym for "crude." We are a civilization of separation and fragmentation, we cannot understand the whole: we separate the mind and the body, nature and its creatures, the spiritual and the beautiful. But when you see a Japanese platter you understand that there can be another way of looking at things, and in this way, nature and manmade beauty don't assert their existence by opposing the other, but by incorporating it. A little plate with a flowerlike arrangement of minuscule orange slices next to a pinch of dark green marinated herbs; another little plate with a brown-green tofu-textured square sprinkled with pink puffed rice; another tiny plate of dark orange pumpkin slices arranged in the shape of a fan with green stripes (the rind); a small plate with a spongy white sphere filled with you-don't-want-to-know-what (some slimy, octopuslike creature popped out when I poked it); a little bowl with four or five rubbery green squares resembling Turkish delight but sprinkled with green tea powder and tasting like seaweed; a goblet filled with what one might call candied walnuts if their taste had been remotely recognizable, but the taste was sweet-and-salty with a touch of something else, entirely unidentifiable; a glazed plate of a turquoise-blue one sees in Mexican folk crafts with a lime-green slice of honeydew melon and two strawberries that tasted like no other fruit you'd ever had.

If you want to understand anything about anyone, look at their food and their gardens. This tells you how they relate to their bodies and the natural world they transform into food, and how they view the relationship between beings and nature. My Sicilian ancestors' mushy polenta says a lot about their *lack of discrimination*. The mush, as a texture, is the poor man's way of incorporating the world, without an eye for its beauty, without the capacity to separate its elements. The French, who think of their food as an expression of an aristocratic sensibility—as opposed to the peasant sensibility of Italian food—are only partially right. True, their sauces, or the liquid-creamy toppings they cover many of their dishes or desserts with, elevate their soon-to-be-ingested products to an artistic experience, but the vision underlying this experience is rather poor. These toppings are decorative, ornamental, like a *stylistic supplement* applied to a pre-existing content. By contrast, Japanese traditional food doesn't see art as a supplement meant to embellish nature; rather, artful shapes are *extracted out of* nature itself in which they exist in latent forms, in the same way Rodin (you know, the French sculptor) used to take a block of marble, and extract—he said—the form hiding inside it. Nowhere else is this vision more visible than in a Japanese garden.

I noticed that No. 4 had been smiling for some time, and when I got to the part on toppings, his smile extended all the way to his ears.

"Yes, I see what you mean. First of all, it was Michelangelo who first said those words about the block of marble—Rodin appropriated them much later." His smile now assuming the impish hue of one who has caught you red-handed, he added, "Second, I too have read Roland Barthes's book on Japan."

"My dear professor, I have no doubt you've read Barthes. I'm sure you are a well read, sophisticated man of letters. As for myself, I'm not in the habit of using other people's thoughts when reflecting on everyday things. I prefer using the inside of the skull Mother Nature has so graciously endowed me with. If you have noticed a certain similarity between whatever Barthes might have said and my words, that's his and your problem."

Having clarified that, I resumed my story. Alma and I arrived one late December afternoon at our *shukubo* in Zenko-ji, so we were forced to wander in the dark through a maze of narrow cobblestone streets lined with wooden *shukubos* and rare lampposts casting pale lights. Each *shukubo* had a tiny front yard with a high wooden fence beyond which you could glimpse a shingled roof and a few bonsai plants and shrubs. I was exhausted and exasperated by our lack of luck in finding our *shukubo*, when I heard Alma's giggle.

"Look," she said, pointing at a sign hanging from a fence with the word "Welcome" followed by our names. Our names on that white sign gracing the upper transverse beam of a carved gateway in the depths of a Japanese night were so incongruous that we began to laugh. We stepped inside the courtyard and walked to the sliding, open front door. At the entrance, there were pairs of shoes and a rack with at least ten umbrellas behind which two wide steps led to the main hall. In the middle of the hall presided a majestic, Buddhalike bronze deity in front of which a plastic plate gathered coin offerings, and a slender vase with an ikebana arrangement held three long stems with tiny, round, purple flowers. We took our shoes off, called, and waited. A woman in her early thirties with a soft, shy smile and a flowery apron appeared immediately. She greeted us in English and saw us to our rooms beyond the blue sliding door with large flower prints. Unlike the rest of the house, which was very cold, our rooms were warm, the floors covered with tatami mats, and the ceiling made of dark cedar square panels along which ran a carved foliated scroll. Our guestroom had a deep recess in one corner where the floor was slightly raised above the mats to accommodate a flower vase, while the rest of the wall on the side of the recess had two big red flowers painted on a greenish background. On the opposite side there was a sliding door opening onto a similar room with two futons next to each other. Each of the futons was covered with two heavy blankets inside white duvet covers, and at their ends a folded cotton yukata and a thick kimono were waiting for us.

With her soft and inviting smile, the woman placed a piece of cloth in a corner of the main room and motioned toward our luggage. Her quiet beauty and serenity seemed an extension of the room's tranquility—or the other way around. We placed our luggage on the piece of cloth, and the woman retreated with two bows and a few words uttered in the rhythm of the bows, like a delicate stammer, a mixture of English and Japanese, a sort of apologetic welcome, as if she was deeply grateful for our being there. I say "as if" because I know that all these manners are simply part of the Japanese ritual of politeness and greeting, and that this woman was not "meek" as our Western eyes see her. And I won't hide from you that I am a lover of rituals and *as ifs*—after all, they represent the fabric of what we call civilization. Even animals have rituals, especially when copulating. They don't just jump on top of each other like animals. The more civilized a society, the more it functions according to predetermined forms and rituals. In this sense, "primitive societies" are the most civilized because they are the most ritualized. The Western world has become a content-only universe. We are all "content-providers." We have forgotten that human exchange, at its best, is based not on content but on form; that is, on ritual.

"Yes, Alma has told me that you are an admirer of 'Japanese quiet beauties,'" the man said with a pathetic attempt at irony.

"Alas, I am more than aware of Alma's sensitivity to what she calls my admiration for 'Japanese quiet beauties.' She is morbidly jealous—and I use the word 'morbid' on purpose. Once, after a particularly vivid scene of jealousy, she chased me throughout the house with a butcher knife.

"Hmm … This is not the Alma *I* know."

"My dear man, this was not the Alma I knew before our marriage, either, but you still have plenty of time to know her. She was immensely jealous of this delightful Japanese woman. Our hostess, I mean. Of course I enjoyed making small talk with her, all the more so since she herself was happy to practice her (quite advanced, I should add) English. And I never made a secret of how thrilled I was to listen to the unexpected turns of her sentences, to the *off* rhythm they embraced, as if embarking on a trip down an unknown river and then resurfacing again, resplendent with the freshness of the magic journey. Listening to such rhythms gives us a pleasure that comes from the deviation from the norm our own language has become to us. Deviation is, by the way, what gives beauty to literary language, too. Deviation within the framework imposed by the words of common usage. Did you know that before I studied architecture I considered becoming a linguist?"

No, he didn't. I told him I committed the imprudence of telling Alma how much I fancy a woman's softness, and how our hostess's movements—combined with her adorable linguistic inadequacies, reminiscent of chopsticks picking a bit of food here, another bit there, like a tongue savoring bits of vowels and textures— were as pleasurable to the eye as our meals. And what was my wife's reaction? The next time our hostess brought us our platters, and before she had time to retreat, my wife took a single chopstick from beside her own plate and, with one of her devilishly provocative smiles, implanted it like a sword into a strawberry-colored, jelly-textured, perfectly molded rectangle—an absolute no-no, the food's stabbing being equated in Japanese culture with death. As she did this, she said, "My husband just loooooves softness. Look how soft this is, honey!" And, lifting the gelatinous rectangle precariously impaled by her chopstick, she brought it to my mouth, trying to force it down my throat. Our hostess was so embarrassed her face turned the color of the jelly.

Ever since, whenever someone uttered the word "soft," Alma would point at me: "He loooves softness." I am not one to explain life stories by some primordial scene, but I am convinced that had we not had that conflict, Alma wouldn't have chosen, a few months later, to return on her own to Japan, and spend another two weeks in the *shukubo* of the Ninna-ji temple. It was a calculated revenge, though fate gave her a hand, too, by putting the right man in the right place.

"Has she talked to you about the young monk?" I asked.

"You mean, the French American monk?"

"Nooo ... I don't mean my predecessor. The young Japanese monk."

"Not really."

"Well, I'm not very surprised. In fact, I anticipated this, and brought you the letter she sent me from there. I don't think I'm committing an indiscretion, since you are now her betrothed, ha, ha. Let's see ... Where is that letter?"

"Here it is. I'm skipping the lovey-dovey stuff; she could be like a barrel of honey when she put her heart in it."

And so I read him the letter, while he was peeking over my shoulder:

It took us forty minutes from the Kyoto train station to reach the temple, which, luckily, was exactly across from the bus stop. The tired winter garden, open to the public and large enough to contain the main hall, the shukubo, the monks' lodging, two old tea houses, two or three public toilets, a pond, a shrine, and at least two locked-up wooden edifices, was closing for the day, and a megaphone blared its announcement in several languages above it. As I crossed the enormous entrance gate guarded by two equally enormous bronze demons, I stopped on the stone stairs, dismayed by the gravel road opening before me. I lifted my suitcase with my last remnants of late-afternoon power and carried it to the first kiosk on the left.

"Ninna-ji Omuro Kaikan doko desu ka?" I asked in my minimal Japanese.

The man, ugly as a character in a Pasolini film, pointed straight ahead. And straight ahead I went. With my suitcase and my backpack I crossed the entire graveled surface, which was no easy feat, climbed a long flight of stairs, and stopped on the paved path between the two main gates of the garden. The thickening winter grayness would soon turn into total darkness, I thought, breathless, looking around in search of something resembling a dwelling. The garden was utterly deserted, and from my standpoint it seemed interminable. As the lengthening night shadows brushed against me, and the metallic voice above me kept blaring, I felt a shiver run down my spine. I was in the middle of nowhere, away from the city, with no one in sight. I was getting ready to shed a few tears of despair when I saw a man with a bundle of keys walk toward me. I heaved a sigh of relief and asked my question again. The man pointed in a different direction than the ugly fellow—a path much closer to the entrance. I lifted my suitcase again, and in less than five minutes I was next to a massive building with large windows through which one could see a souvenir shop on the ground floor and peach-colored armchairs with coffee tables in between. I paused for a second to catch my breath and to better enjoy the warmth emanating from the lodging, its human touch that contrasted with the cold outside. When I attempted to lift my luggage again, my hand grasped the air.

"May I help you?" I heard a voice next to me, and when I looked, a Japanese man in a monk's garb had already taken my luggage and was carrying it hurriedly. I followed him inside—it was warm and cozy, in spite of the large hall.

The monk put my suitcase down, and in the light I could see that he was very young—twenty-one, twenty-three years old at most—and quite handsome. His head was shaved in the traditional way, and his features were very pure, almost childlike. This purity was accentuated by a barely sensual smile and the intensity in his eyes, whose gaze had a Jesuitlike ambivalence, manly and childish at the same time. He measured me—in a rather unmonkish way, I should add—and began to explain the house rules in a patient, even voice, punctuated by that charming smile. I realized that he was the monk in charge of the lodging and the guests, and I was more than happy to let myself be tended to by such a representative of the male species. On the left wall, he explained, were the shelves where the guests were supposed to leave their shoes, and from where they could pick their slippers. In front, the souvenir shop was open as long as there was someone at the front desk. On the right, the restaurant where one could have breakfast and dinner.

While we were talking, two men walked past us, shuffling their slippers as they checked out the souvenirs in the shop, most of them Japanese cakes with bean paste, or dried weird sea creatures. That was the first time the sound of shuffling, slippered feet struck me as profoundly unpleasant, probably because it was on a background of soft classical music. From then on, this sound would follow me everywhere, from the restroom to the bathroom, the corridors, the restaurant and the lounge area, always produced by Japanese middle-aged men or women who had as a common denominator a striking ugliness and a very provincial air. They seemed to be part of a self-sufficient universe whose characteristics were more aesthetic than ethnic, to the point that they could have been Russian, I thought, visualizing the characters in a Chekhov play.

Later that evening, while enjoying the peach-hued comfort of one of the armchairs with a novel in my lap and the corner of my right eye on the Japanese man standing in front of the souvenir shop trying to decide between two plastic pouches with an unidentifiable content, I had the feeling that the theater of life was so universal that, if I wanted, I could understand the dialogue of the two women seated across from me, who had arrived with the man. (I remembered what you once said about life being ritual and not content, and that it's when speaking in a foreign language, or speaking our own language with a foreigner that we begin to comprehend how grounded in theater and ritual our lives are.) Not really understand their words, but figure out the meaning from their expressions and gestures. They had arrived together from an upstairs floor, all three of them in the white, blue-striped yukata covered by the khaki woolen kimono, and the green slippers provided by our hosts, the two women ostensibly related to the man in different ways. Judging from their ages, one must have been his mother, and the other his wife. Both had old-fashioned hair styles, short and puffed-up, as common in the sixties, and both looked like the kind of women who spend their afternoons cooking laborious meals and browsing glossy magazines on home design. Their teeth were very crooked, and their drooping features oozed the androgynous flat air of countless middle-aged housewives around the planet. Their chatter and shuffling of feet had disturbed my reading—by the way, it's a mystery to me why Japanese people seem incapable of walking properly in slippers, considering how much practice they must have—and since I couldn't go back to my book, I couldn't stop eavesdropping.

"Only twenty minutes left until the restaurant opens." (Mother)

"Yes, that's right." (Wife)

"I can hardly wait to see what's on the menu." (Mother)

"Yes, me too. Remember last year? We had some great meals here." (Wife)

"Yes, yes, I remember. How could I forget?" (Mother)

"I wonder what's taking [man's name] so long." (Wife, turning her head in the direction of the man in front of the souvenir shop) "What are you doing there? What are you buying again?"

"Some fish chips for myself and a present for … I'm waiting for the store clerk to return with my change." (Man)

"He's buying fish chips." (Wife to Mother, both laughing) "Since you are there, get me some cinnamon cookies!"

A minute later, the man returns with three plastic pouches, of which he gives one to his wife.

"Only fifteen minutes left until the restaurant opens." (Man, after consulting his watch)

"Twelve minutes." (Mother)

"Twelve, fifteen, whatever. I'm starving." (Man)

"Did you see there are foreigners here?" (Wife, eyeing the Caucasian woman in front of her) "This place must be world-famous."

"It's certainly an important cultural asset. People from all over the world come to see it." (Mother)

"These chips aren't bad." (Man) "Would you like some?" (to Mother)

"You shouldn't eat before dinner!" (Mother)

The Man closes the bag of chips and looks again at his watch:

"Only ten minutes left."

"Should we go downtown tonight to see the illuminations?" (Wife)

"Of course we should!" (Man)

"Are you sure? We won't finish dinner before seven-thirty, and by the time we are there it will be after eight. Doesn't the whole thing end at nine?" (Mother)

"We'll still have an hour." (Man)

"I think I'd like to rest." (Wife)

"You always want to rest." (Man)

"I'd rather take a bath than go out." (Mother)

"Very well, then. I'll go by myself." (Man)

Of course it is more than possible that what they were saying was entirely different; but they were most certainly waiting for the restaurant to open. The man was not unattractive—he had the high cheekbones and dark sideburns of an Italian actor from the neorealist period—but there was something off-putting about his demeanor, maybe his slacked body, maybe his shuffling feet, maybe the very existence of the two women sitting in those chairs like two hens with clipped wings.

Finally, the restaurant door opened, and the threesome jumped as one from their armchairs and rushed to the door. The food was even more impressive than at our shukubo in Nagano. There were about six parties sitting on cushions before low tables with room numbers on them. The younger couples were in their street clothes, but the middle-aged and the older ones were in kimonos and yukatas. Once again, I noticed the difference between the younger and the older generations, visible like a yellow line dividing a city in two. The youngsters looked like young people everywhere, but the elderly were from a different century, with deep wrinkles like engravings in a tree bark, and hunched backs that had never entered a gym. You see the same difference between generations on the streets in Europe; our country alone seems to live in an eternal present, with the older generations merely a less-perfect version of the younger ones, as if people, too, like objects, had to obey the rules of technological progress and be constantly up-to-date. But I'm starting to talk like Patrice.... Have you seen her lately, by the way?

Let's go back to the two women and their man, who had just finished their dinner. The women walked up to their room, and the man went out. As for myself, I decided to check out the bathroom. Remember the big bathtub in our shukubo? Well, this one was as big as a pool. The anteroom itself was large and airy, with towels and baskets to place your clothes in. Then, past a sliding door, you entered the dark green ceramic-tiled bathroom, where, through steam as dense as in a Turkish bath, you could make out the blurry outline of a triangular-shaped, enormous tub that covered half the room. Along the right wall were showers, and in front of the room were plastic stools one could use while showering. If you've seen old Japanese postcards, you might have seen images with such baths in which some women bathe, others soap themselves or wash their undergarments while sitting on a stool, and others shower before getting into the water. You know the ritual: soap, shower, bathe.

I took my clothes off in a heartbeat and, since I had the place all to myself, I circumvented the ritual and plunged into the water. It was so hot I thought my skin would boil. But once you got used to it, it was divine, soaking in that liquid fire that melted your senses and set your brains ablaze, with nothing but bluish steam around you, rising like mist above a lake, and you were all at once the lake, the mist, and the nothingness separating them. I was enjoying that state of joyful brainlessness when I heard voices around me, and, opening my eyes, I saw the two women from the lounge stark naked, getting into the tub with me. Needless to say, they ruined my enjoyment, and I wanted to get out of the water, but didn't want to appear rude, so I decided to stay a little longer. Their bodies were not the most attractive expression of nakedness, but they couldn't care less. (It seems that Japanese women are less modest than we are.) They were of average weight, the younger one more on the skinny side, but their muscles weren't toned and their skin was flabby. When two little girls, who appeared out of nowhere, jumped into the water with us, I took advantage of the splash and got out.

Later that evening I was back in the lounge, my skin still pink and hot, smelling of lavender lotion, with that cotton robe wrapped around me, and the woolen kimono on top. And, yes, I was wearing those silly green slippers of theirs, with my sky-blue microfiber socks, soft as the fabric in that softener commercial with the bear. I was back in the same armchair as before, with the same novel in my hands—*The Makioka Sisters*, which, as you know, I'd started numerous times in the past and never got beyond the first hundred pages of. But this time I was determined to finish it. The cellular memory of the hot bath I'd taken and the softness in which my entire being was sunk in that armchair merged in one thread of pure pleasure, as if the melting from the tub was being continued in a different element. Wrapped in that amniotic-fluid-like softness, like a cat in its own fur, I was almost purring with pleasure when I heard a masculine voice utter in English with a mild Japanese accent:

"That must be a very good book. You seem so absorbed...."

I raised my head and saw the Japanese man (now orphaned of the two women) who was, very likely, returning from downtown. You know how much I hate being interrupted when I read. Besides, he himself had noticed how 'absorbed' I was—then why in the world would he disturb me? I didn't want to encourage him, so I kept my mouth shut and just pointed at the title.

"Tanizaki!" He exclaimed, with more enthusiasm than I anticipated. "He is one of my favorite authors...."

Now, he seemed unstoppable. It was clear he wanted to share his love of Tanizaki, so he promptly sat down in the armchair next to mine. He works in advertising, he said, but dreams of opening a language school one day. And wouldn't I like to work for him, if he did? I said I have to ask my husband first.

The next day I was sitting again in the lounge—a different armchair. It was shortly after lunch and the place was empty, with only the young monk at the front desk. A piece of classical music was playing softly in the background: melodic, but not too intense, allowing one to concentrate on something else.

'Hmm ... Excuse me.'

I looked up and saw the young monk, shy as a bride, with his rosebud-smile reddening his lips.

"Eerrmm ... Our cook would like to know if you'd like to have some tea."

"Sure. Thank you."

The young monk's lashes, as long as those of a cute toddler, fluttered rapidly over his half-closed eyes.

As soon as he left, the cook was next to me with a lacquered platter, a tea pot, and two cups.

"Oh, I don't need two cups," I said, but the cook didn't seem to understand and walked away.

A minute later, the young monk was back with a brick-thick book under his arm.

"I brought you a book about the temples of Kyoto," he said with the same butterfly effect of the lashes. "You may take it to your room."

I took the book and thanked him, and, as my gaze fell on the two cups, I said, "Would you like to join me for a cup of tea?"

This time, the eyelash flutter was preceded by a brief hesitation. He then sat down with the same gentle awkwardness as our hostess from Nagano—I'm sure you haven't forgotten *her*!—but which in his case was a hundred times more appealing. Well, I'm afraid I have to stop here for now. You'll get an account of our conversation in another letter, if I am moved to write it down.

Alma

"I don't think I ever got a full account of this, or any of her other conversations with the young monk, but I do know," I said on finishing the letter, "and this from the horse's mouth, that they have written to each other regularly and he has invited her repeatedly to return. There would always be a room for her there. And the maple trees lining the path between the *shukubo* and the main alley whose leaves are as red as her hair would always wait for her. I am not making this stuff up: *he* wrote it in one of those carefully crafted English composition masterpieces he sent her on light-blue handmade paper. By the way, Alma's hair is black, but never mind."

"Are you saying you read her letters?"

"Of course I read them—who do you take me for? The French monk?! At least I read those I could get my hands on, and I'm sure there were many more. Do you see what I'm getting at? That's where she is, at Ninna-ji, hiding behind that monk's robe. To tell you the truth, I'm glad she left *you* for a monk."

"She didn't leave me ..."

"No, let me finish! She may come back, yes, but she did leave you, let's face it! I mean, you haven't seen her in ... how long? Three weeks? As I was saying, I'm glad she left *you* for a monk because it would have been much too ironic for her to leave *me* for him after she'd left another monk for me."

"She didn't leave me, she just ..."

"Yes, I get your point: she didn't leave you, she just disappeared. Well, in that case, tell me: what does her disappearance mean? Do you suspect foul play? Because if she hasn't left you, she was ... what? Murdered? Kidnapped?"

"Please don't say that!"

"What do you want me to say? Did you alert the police? Oh, you didn't. May I ask why?"

"As long as the police aren't involved, I can still believe that nothing bad has happened."

"Let me tell you something: if something bad *did* happen, you'd be the first suspect."

"I thought *you*'d know where she is."

"Why would you think that? Don't you know she left me nine months ago? For all I know she might have left me for you."

"She left you because you were violent and she was afraid of you."

"Did *she* tell you that?! I never laid a finger on her! Well, yes, I did raise my voice at her, so what? Since when is raising one's voice 'violence'? Silence can be violent too, you know. There is nothing more violent than hostile silence. The hostile silence of a moody wife sitting in an armchair like a maiden awaiting her martyrdom. Alma was very good at that, though she was even better at speaking her mind. She spoke her mind constantly, up and down, right and left. Her mind was everywhere: in our bed, our fridge, our living room. The only place you couldn't find it was in her head. Never again will I get involved with an 'intelligent woman'! They are the stupidest of all. If I am insane enough to get remarried, I'll get myself a healthy peasant woman whose mind and body are always where they are supposed to be: the former in her head and the latter in bed. I spent a fortune on Alma's shrinks, and in the end, what good did it do? So she can accuse me of wanting to kill her? Yes, in one of her paranoid attacks she accused me of plotting to kill her. To top it off, she used something she'd learned from me, a creation myth from the Balkans."

He was curious to hear what the myth was about, and so I told him.

In the myth, a mason—unable to complete the monastery he was building during the day, which was being destroyed by an unknown force at night, and having dreamed one night that the only way to finish it was by walling up in the construction itself the first human being who'd show up the next morning—sacrifices his pregnant wife. Full of grief, he begins to immure his wife, pretending he's playing a game. As the wall rises up to her knees, and then to her waist, she tells him that the child is crying inside her. Seeing that the wall is up to her breasts, and that this is no joke, she begs him to stop, but he doesn't, and then the wall covers her up, and the mason keeps hearing the sobs from behind it. He finishes the monastery, which is the most beautiful monastery ever built, and when the Black King—who had ordered the construction—asks him whether he could build another one just as beautiful, he proudly answers that he could make an even more dazzling one. So the king, jealous that another sovereign might use the mason to erect a monastery that would compete with his, decides to abandon him and his men on top of the building. The mason and his men then construct wooden wings to help them fly away from there, but, like Icarus, they all fall to the ground, and as they do, a spring of the purest water shoots up.

"Do you know anything wiser ever said about the act of creation?" I asked, but didn't wait for his answer, which, frankly, didn't interest me. "To create is to sacrifice yourself and everything you love. To sacrifice, *and not to kill!* Because Alma got it into her head that I wanted to kill her in order to create my magnum opus!"

I remembered how she once said, toward the end of our marriage, when we were arguing every day:

"I know you would have walled me up inside *his* (the French Monk's, that is) tower, but you couldn't, not with him there. What better opportunity for you to exercise your black magic, which you call art, than to create a Love Tower for a monk, and to literally immure within the symbol itself the woman to whom it's dedicated?"

At first I thought she was kidding. By then, she'd gone through several shrinks and was spending all her time staring at a wall. Maybe that's how she got the idea. If you stare at a wall long enough, you begin to identify with it—ha, ha! At the end of our marriage, she even accused me of having built on purpose "that monstrosity" in order to destroy her marriage with the Monk.

"By the way," I asked No. 4, "have you seen the tower I'm talking about?"

He hadn't, he replied. The Monk was already living in an apartment when he'd seen him.

"Yes, I know. The house is for sale."

I told him that that "monstrosity," as Alma calls it, is in fact a scaled-down version of what the Monk had in mind at the time. He'd wanted not only a much taller tower, but he'd wanted it in the middle of his living room. I convinced him that it was aesthetically more enticing and architecturally more sound to build the tower outside, snuggled against the front wall of the house, and tall enough to communicate with the mansard loft. This was, in fact, the hardest part, as I had to figure out a way of linking the spiral staircase with the loft. I came up with a wooden platform from which a flight of regular stairs led up to the loft. We decided to use granite boulders for the tower to match the lower half of the house. Luckily, here, the Monk and I were in perfect agreement: he liked the idea of the boulders, because it suggested permanence, and he chose the stone himself, making sure it had a certain pink vein running through it.

Oh, I understood very well what the Monk wanted. I understood only too well and I pitied him. In a different century he would have ordered, like the Black King, the construction of a church or a monastery, and dedicated it to a saint, but now, after he'd lost his church, he wanted to erect the closest thing: a tower dedicated to a woman. What he didn't know when he lost his church is that God is a much safer investment than a woman. I always thought he'd go back to the monastery after the divorce, but he didn't. Well, maybe I was wrong. Maybe God himself isn't a very safe investment either.

But the reason I enjoyed building the Monk's tower was, in fact, personal, and it had to do with my philosophy as an architect. We normally don't think of space as a natural conduit for rhythm, we only associate time with rhythmical flow. The oscillation of a clock's hands or the sound of a tick-tock are representations of time as rhythm. If we had to live in a shapeless time, that is, in an eternal, undivided present, we'd probably go mad. But we don't think in the same way about space, and maybe we should. It may be that to attain a state of relative mental equilibrium we'd have to inhabit a space governed by the laws of rhythm. Alma's attraction to monasteries and temples is based on a healthy intuition—namely, one that senses the effect of space on our mental state. Monasteries and temples are created on the premise that our inner and exterior spaces are a continuation of each other, and that time and space are two dimensions that should follow the same rhythm—that is, if we want to live in harmony. Everything in a monastery has the same rhythm, starting with the building itself, erected according to architectural patterns that channel a rhythmical flow. For instance, what first grabs your attention when you enter an old monastery are the rows of columns, whose purpose isn't only practical—that is, a means of support—or aesthetic. If you pay attention, you can see that the flow is marked by the number of solid spaces (the columns) and the voids in between them. Some historians of art have compared the solid spaces to stressed syllables and the voids to unstressed ones, as if the space in its entirety were a poem or a piece of music. Of course, in our Western perception the focus is on the solid or stressed space, while for a Japanese, it's the void that gives meaning to the space, or rather, the lack of meaning signified by the void isn't unsettling, as it is for us. We are frightened by emptiness, and cannot rest until we fill it: with stuff or words, whatever, as long as it alleviates our paralysis before the Great Void. Japanese space is meaningful through the emptiness that inhabits its core; in other words, it is wonderfully meaning*less*. That's why Japanese people aren't scared of silence, the way we are, and aren't trying to fill it with empty words.

At this, No. 4 asked if by emptiness I meant the lack of furniture in the rooms. I smiled:

"Not necessarily, though it's true that our rooms are much more cluttered than theirs. Think of Japanese space as a novel in which the main character is absent. Normally, the main character is the center around which everything else evolves. Try to imagine a novel in which the story develops around an absence. The Western version of such a novel would be the murder mystery or the detective story that starts with a killing. But in this version, the killing is already a presence, the presence of the corpse that signifies the absence of the victim, so the novel is the adventure of turning the absence inside-out like a jacket, turning it into a meaningful—that is, brimming with meaning—story. The story focuses on finding the killer and thus on filling the absence, or the corpse, with meaning. Well, try to imagine a novel in which the killer is never found, and in which there is no corpse, and the victim's disappearance is based on the presumption of a killing that is never proved. Such a novel would be centered on an absence that is never filled with meaning."

"Hmm, I'm trying to follow what you're saying, but it seems to me that such a novel wouldn't care much about someone like me," he observed with a somewhat bitter smile.

I was so focused on the thread of my own thoughts I didn't get his point right away. He seemed like a good listener with a cranium developed well enough to engage with my architectural theories, so rather than wasting time I resumed elucidating my own thoughts:

"Our contemporary world seems particularly oblivious to the necessities of inner peace when it comes to structuring space. We live in rectangular boxes within a circular flow of time. Wouldn't it make more sense to live inside round spaces? Try to imagine living in a world in which not only would our rooms be circular but streets, buses, nay, everything would also have curved, rather than angular, lines. It makes you dizzy, doesn't it? Well, this is the world I want to build, and the Monk's tower was the best practice for it. I'm trying to get funds for an experimental town, Round Point. The name is a play on a French expression, *le rond point*, which refers to a circular area where roads converge in a city. If we lived in circular spaces, our entire inner rhythm would be different. To begin with, we would no longer live with the permanent conflict between circular time and rectangular space. Our visions of time and space would, finally, reunite. I bet this would solve most cases of depression, which probably wouldn't make doctors happy. In fact, I tried to convince Alma that I could cure her depression if she agreed to participate in such an experiment. I asked her to live for a while in the tower I'd built for the Monk, but she reacted with such violence that I never dared renew my proposal. This was after the Monk had moved out of the house, but before he'd put it on the market. She was livid with anger, saying that it was monstrous of me to propose such a thing. Later, when our marriage was in shreds, she got back to this, saying that it was a sign I had never loved her, because no one would want his wife to go back to such a psychologically charged space. But she didn't understand that this sort of childish symbolism meant nothing to me. What counts for me is the reality of a space, which makes its mark on our minds. I really wanted to help her."

I recounted how one evening I was at my desk, engrossed in my work, when I had the uncomfortable feeling that a pair of unfriendly eyes were piercing my back, so I turned my head, and there she was, in the leather armchair in my office, staring at me with a hateful gaze that distorted her face almost beyond recognition.

"Don't you imagine for a second that I don't know what you are up to!" she spewed out between clenched teeth.

"What am I up to?"

"Don't you play innocent with me!"

"What are you talking about, woman?"

She hated it when I called her "woman": furious, she threw a shoe at me, calling me "murderer."

"Why are you calling me 'murderer'?" I asked, dodging the shoe.

"Because that's what you are. You can be a murderer before actually committing the crime."

"And what crime am I going to commit?"

She didn't answer, but kept staring at me with the same hateful look, then hissed through her teeth:

"Murderer!"

At that moment, she looked like a snake. And I confess that I would have loved to crush her under my foot the way you do with a snake, but instead I tried to keep my cool: "Could you be more specific in your accusations?"

"If you think that you can just make me disappear so you can propel yourself into immortality you've chosen the wrong sacrificial victim. I've already spoken with Nora and with a friend who is a policeman. *People have their eyes on you.* You can't simply make me vanish behind a wall."

I was so stunned I didn't know what to say. I just stared at her, dumbstruck, and she stared back at me with that inscrutable face, but quietly, as if she was beginning to realize the enormity of her accusation. But the truth is I have no idea what was going through her mind, whether she was sorry for what she'd said or, on the contrary, whether my silence convinced her that she was right.

The next day I called Nora.

"Your sister is behaving strangely," I began. "Last night she accused me of—guess what? Of wanting to kill her."

There was no reply at the other end. The silence was so thick I thought the connection must have been cut or Nora must have hung up. But when I said, "Hello," she answered right away. "Yes, I'm here."

"And ..."

And nothing. Nora was silent again. For the moment, I was simply confounded, but in retrospect, her reaction seems highly suspicious. That was not the normal way anyone would react to such a statement. She acted as if she were already in on it. Could she really believe that I wanted to kill Alma?!

I had uttered the sentence above in a rhetorical way, but, surprisingly, No. 4 answered:

"Maybe she didn't *really* believe that, but she thought you were responsible for Alma's breakdown, and so, indirectly, that you wanted to kill her."

"Do *you* think I was responsible for Alma's breakdown?"

Silence. A very talkative silence, as Alma would say. So, that's where I stood.

"Frankly, I'm really sorry you won't have a chance to be her lawful groom, because I would have loved to see you a year from now. I would have loved to see your face scratched by her wild cat's claws, your brain shaken like a yo-yo at a children's party. You should consider yourself lucky that she left you now. She'd drive you to your grave. Just pray she'll stay away long enough so you may cancel the wedding without appearing too crass. She ..."

With every word I uttered, my vision turned blurrier and blurrier, and my head lighter and lighter until, the anger having gone all to my head, so to speak, I was no longer steady on my legs.

"I'm sorry, I have to sit down. My heart ... I have a heart condition. Could you please bring me a glass of water?"

When he returned—his face trying to show concern, which was nice of him, even if he didn't really care—and after I downed the water, I said:

"Forget everything I told you. It doesn't matter. Just go look for her at Ninna-ji. I know she is with that young monk. How do I know it? I just know."

"How can they allow this in a temple?" No. 4 said, barely concealing his fury.

"No, no, it's not a temple, it's a *shukubo*, which is no more sacred than a bed and breakfast. And you have to realize that the Japanese don't have our Western prejudices. Alma told me that not only were people free to smoke at the Ninna-ji *shukubo*, they could also buy cigarettes at the front desk. The young monk was probably a smoker himself. By the way, I once found a photo of him in one of Alma's books. Quite charming, but not manly at all. I can see *him* infatuated with her, but Alma … Did you talk to Nora?"

He shook his head: no.

"I'm sure she has a fresh perspective on all this. Alma confides in her sister, though she despises her. She tells her things she doesn't tell anyone else because, as she once put it, 'Nora is like a bright horizon to which I can open my heart at the end of a tough day without having to worry about the consequences, because every word falls into the void.'

"Yes, you have to talk to Nora, though I wouldn't trust her. At least with Alma you know where you stand. There was a time when I thought Nora was quite fond of me—to the point that I began to suspect she had a crush on me. Once, shortly after her divorce from what's-his-name, when Alma was gone on one of her trips abroad, Nora invited me to have dinner at her place, saying that she'd forgotten she was divorced and had cooked for two, and besides, with Alma being gone, I needed a woman to take care of me.

"Now, I have a principle: I never refuse a dinner invitation, especially when it comes from someone who can cook better than my better half, and, alas, anyone can cook better than Alma. I am not saying this to be mean. Alma has plenty of fine qualities but, as I'm sure you've noticed, cooking is not one of them."

"I think her cooking is just fine."

"Well, to each his own standards.... At any rate, I gladly accepted Nora's invitation, thinking that it would do us both good; she, after a bitter divorce, and I, symbolically widowed by my wife's fancy for Japanese monks. I was a bit surprised to find Nora in a cocktail dress with a very low cleavage and a voluminous pearl necklace forcing one's gaze to land and linger on the neighboring skin. The table was festively set, with two slender candles on each side of a vase with red roses, and a bright white tablecloth with a rich lacework that reminded me of my grandmother's embroidered napkins. Nora was tense in a way I'd never seen her before, as if she hadn't known me for three or however many years. At first, I thought she wanted to tell me something about Alma, and since Nora is the kind of woman who needs a special 'atmosphere' for every situation in life, I imagined that she just needed all that theater as a prop for our discussion. By the way, have you ever read any of her novels?"

"No."

"Well, I read one. Very instructive. 'Every time she thought of him, a tangled, woolly longing came over her, so she took up knitting, and by the end of the winter she'd knitted away several woolen scarves of frustrated desire.' Actually, only the first half is a quote; I kind of made up the ending. But it makes you understand how all female activities are nothing but substitutes for sexual desire."

"Don't you think one could say the same thing about male activities?"

"Hmm … Do you know of any male activities consisting of a repetitive, mechanical, rhythmical movement—like knitting?"

"Woodcutting?"

"Well, *my* people haven't done any woodcutting in several generations, ha, ha!

"So, there we were, Nora and I, eating her delicious pork roast with apple sauce, and making conversation like two idiots on their first date. I kept waiting for her to spit out whatever it was she wanted to tell me, but in vain. We had drunk a whole bottle of red wine and, as I took out my pipe and sat on the couch, comfortably settling into my postdinner mode, she walked up to the window and, with a languorous gesture, rested her right cheek on the curtains, looked out, and murmured in that 'sultry voice' of hers (as one of her characters would say):

"'Oh, look at the moon! The moon is full tonight!'

"I had no intention to look at the moon in that moment, as that would have entailed my getting up and leaving the couch, with which I felt in perfect harmony. But she didn't seem bothered by my lack of reaction, because she went on:

"'It looks like a crystal ball hanging in the dark night of our souls and illuminating it with its prophecies.'

"I had just taken a long, satisfying puff, and I felt I had to say something to show that I was paying attention, so I said:

"'Possible.'

"But she seemed totally engrossed in her contemplation and continued without paying me any heed:

"'Or like a ball left by a child in the thick of the night, a lonely ball bouncing inside the bowels of the indifferent universe.'

"Now I really didn't know what to answer, so I didn't say anything. Luckily, she stopped there and, leaving her meditation spot, came near the couch and sat down on the rug in front of it, with one elbow propped on the couch and her head resting on her right arm. We sat like that for a few seconds in silence until she asked:

"'Have you heard from Alma lately?'

"'No, actually, I haven't.'

"'Well, maybe she's too busy hanging out with that Japanese man.'

"She said the last sentence barely audibly, and I wasn't sure I'd heard well.

"'You mean that young monk?'

"'Oh no, I mean the Japanese man she'd met at Ninna-ji, the man who was traveling with his wife and his mother.'

"I remembered the threesome Alma had described in her first letter from Ninna-ji, but she'd never mentioned that man again. *Well, this is an interesting development*, I thought. And then, out loud:

"'So, she told you she was going to meet that man ...'

"With her left hand, Nora began to draw some circles on the couch, and with her mouth buried in her right arm, she mumbled:

"'Oh, she wasn't sure ... She said he was a little strange, and she had ambivalent feelings about him: on the one hand, she was scared by the dark, wild spark in his eyes, but on the other hand, she found that attractive. And she didn't know whether she could believe anything he said, because he was so elusive about his job.'

"'So, is she at Ninna-ji now?'

"'Oh, I don't know.' Nora's head moved uncertainly, with her eyes closed, as if she were going to fall asleep at any moment. 'I think they decided to meet in a different city, closer to where he lived.'

"'So, what's her relationship,' I began, but before I could add 'with this man,' her head fell heavily into my lap, and her arms embraced my legs. I tapped her lightly on the shoulder, but she didn't stir, and a few seconds later I could hear the regular rhythm of her breathing.

"After this encounter, whenever our paths crossed, she was stiff and distant, as if I had wronged her somehow. Once, when I alluded to the Japanese man, she pretended she had no idea what I was talking about. I concluded that she was embarrassed by her … performance that night, but later I came to understand that it was more than that; that, in fact, she held a grudge against me. When Alma had her breakdown during the last months of our marriage, she stayed with Nora, and each time I called, Nora answered the phone in an annoyed tone, giving me vague and hostile answers when I inquired about Alma. They formed an alliance that, more than by their blood ties, was solidified by their hostility against me, as if they had finally discovered a common passion. After a while, the enmity grew into a war: Nora simply refused to tell me anything about Alma or even put her on the phone, claiming that I was harming her mental recovery. And then, one day, I found a divorce notice in my mailbox. If there is anyone who should get credit for my divorce, it is the Evil Sister. There is nothing worse than a resentful woman intent on punishing a man for having witnessed her weakness. And when the woman hides under an excessively feminine appearance, like Nora, you can be in for a surprise! She, with her caramel curls bouncing around her virginal neck, and her heart-shaped mouth ululating pink-inflected sentences like, 'The sky has retreated behind a foreboding brass orchestra' (when it rains and thunders); or, 'The park was invaded by colorful, Pottery Barn strollers hosting an army of open mouths whose cries tore apart the light of day' (to describe a scene with suburban mothers and crying babies); or, 'After forty years, they were still united by a wet placenta of mistrustful tears and umbilical guilt' (about a mother-daughter relationship). Who in his right mind talks (or writes) like this? You wouldn't believe how many idiots love this stuff! Oh, I just remembered another great one: 'Her menstrual blood was the Holy Grail waiting at the end of his night-long labyrinths.' The scary thing is that if you read enough of this stuff, it becomes contagious. You start to speak like a character in her novels: 'I was walking toward the musty grayness of my office, full with the bleak lethargy of a purulent Monday morning.' She has a fondness for liquid metaphors. Have you noticed that?"

"I told you I haven't read her. Have you ever talked about literature and writing with Nora?"

"I don't know.... I've talked about many things with Nora."

"And?"

"For Nora, writing a novel is like playing hopscotch. The only thing the novelist has to come up with is the specific permutation, which in turn needs to be dressed in its Sunday best. But maybe writing, like all artistic creation, is, on the contrary, dressed in Monday clothing. It is never fulfillment, always absence, Mondayed-absence turned toward the already-gone-Sunday."

"I have a feeling you are secretly writing."

"Secretly? Why secretly? I don't do anything secretly. I write and publish essays. But if you mean that I have 'writerly' aspirations, no! Thank God!"

"In that case, one could ask what gives you the authority to speak with such conviction about writing?"

"What gives me the authority is having attempted to do the same thing any writer does: to create something out of nothing. Well, any writer who doesn't play hopscotch."

"Are you sure that what you do is 'create something out of nothing'? After all, you work with materials: stone, wood, whatever."

"That's not the point. A writer works with ink and paper, too."

"It's not the same thing. A writer doesn't transform that paper into something else. You, on the other hand, take stone and make it into something else."

"I *make* a house out of stone, but I *create* it out of nothing. *Before,* there was nothing; *after,* there is something. But to come back to Nora, her writings are the perfect example of the divorce between form and content in the modern world. For her, form is cosmetics; ornament, the cherry she lays on top of her 'story' to, supposedly, embellish it. There was a time when beauty and virtue weren't separated, when form and content were united into a cosmos that signified cosmetics, or ornament, *and* order, at the same time. A *cosm-ethics.* Ornament wasn't simply the cherry on top, but the rhythm sustaining the entire whole. In architecture that meant that the building was *ordered*—that is, organized, put in order—according to certain mathematical rules of proportion, which gave it rhythm and elevated it to a creation that transcended its utilitarian content."

"Did you and Alma ever talk about architecture and creation?"

"Alma has always created a knot where there had been nothing before. It was uncanny how the smallest thing, the tiniest speck of dust, would get caught in the crossfire of our conversation, solidifying like a pearl inside a shell, except it was no pearl, but, rather, its opposite. What's the opposite of a pearl? A small turd, I guess.

"But to return to Nora: this purulent Eve, this snakesse, this gangrene with the appearance of a succulent apple managed to poison my marriage. Like a worm into an apple, she burrowed her way into my mind and made me suspicious of Alma's words and actions. When Alma returned from her trip, I questioned her more harshly than I should have about the Japanese older man and the young monk, and this only made her retreat even more stubbornly into her coiled silence. Meanwhile, Nora was the puppetmaster pulling the strings behind the curtains. I wouldn't be surprised if she convinced Alma to go away and hide from you. I'm sure she knows where Alma is hiding. She'll deny it, of course, but you'd be a fool to believe her. Yes, go and talk to Nora!"

Nora

Of course I knew he'd been talking to all her exes. I always know whensomething concerning Alma is going on. In spite of our differences, Alma and I are like complementary twins: opposite in many ways, but twins nonetheless. I can sense when she has a problem. During the last months of her marriage with the Architect I was in a constant state of anxiety, even before she told me how bad things were.

"I'm so glad you finally came," I told him. "I don't even know where to start."

In reply, No. 4 looked at me in a way that left no doubt: he'd already talked to the Architect. I could tell from his cloudy gaze, as if a new layer of murky knowledge had been deposited onto his innocent eyes. I told him as much:

"I know you've already talked to the Architect!"

After he acknowledged this, I added:

"Some story he must have told you! I won't hide it from you: I fear for Alma's life, and you should too! He's a dangerous man, you should have realized that! Unless he bewitched you—

he's very good at turning things upside down, at taking the facts and coating them with a glossy paint so in the end all you can see is a thick layer of veneer and nothing underneath."

He fixed his cloudy gaze on me again, and I could tell he was still intoxicated with the Architect's speech. *No point in forcing things*, I thought. *Let's give him some time.* So I changed the subject:

"Have you met the Monk? The French monk, I mean. Alma made a huge mistake when she left him. He ad*ooooo*red her. And she was very much in love with him, too, but then No. 3 appeared at one of those times when she was … well, you know, all it takes is for one to show up at the right time and to say what may seem like the right thing at the moment. And the Architect is good at that! Talking and talking … That's what he did with Patrice, too. Poor Patrice! Have you met her? No?! You *have* to meet Patrice!

"God, I don't even know where to start! I'm so glad I can finally talk to you! You have to understand that Alma is in really bad shape. That is, if she is … if she is still alive."

He was sitting on the edge of the couch as if he was ready to take off at any moment, with his coat still on. At that moment he interrupted me, asking if I knew where Alma was.

"No, I don't know where she is. What makes you think I do? Well, a month ago I *did* know where she was. I can't tell you where, but she was out of the country. And she was going to come back, but then she just vanished. I called the place where she was staying and they told me that she'd left."

"Please, you have to tell me where she's been. Otherwise, how can I ever find her? It may be a question of life and death."

I didn't let him beg much. After all, in a question of life and death a promise may be broken.

"Well, since you insist, it was in a *shukubo* in Japan. But she left! She left almost a month ago."

He got up to take his coat off, and, while he struggled with it in the most ungainly way—I confess I never thought much of Alma's taste in men, save for the French Monk, of course—he kept talking to himself like someone not quite right in the head. All I could make out was "Why would she do that? I don't understand …"

"I think it all started with a tent—the tent Father gave her for her eleventh birthday. Every day she'd spend hours in that tiny, hot, dark dwelling, like a fetus in a womb, with her favorite doll by her side, Betty. As soon as she entered the tent her behavior changed: she'd speak only in a whisper, as if afraid of dispelling some magic, as if the tent was a sacred circle that imposed a secret set of rules. The tent became her hiding place during her teenage years, and it gave her, I think, a desire to retreat to a safe abode away from the world. That's why, when the French Monk began to build that tower, I thought that, finally, Alma's ideal home would become one and the same with her real one—but what happened was just the opposite. It made her run away again. By the way, have you seen the tower?"

He shook his head: no.

"You *have* to see it! It's quite impressive, something to behold! A bizarre work of architecture—sometimes I wonder whether the Architect did that on purpose. I mean, whether he built it in order to alienate Alma from her home and the Monk. Poor Monk! One of the handsomest men I've ever seen, yet he has no idea how handsome he is, and as a consequence doesn't know how to take advantage of it. Isn't it strange how Nature sometimes gives the power of seduction to people who aren't even attractive? I'm talking about the Architect, of course. This man thinks that no woman can resist him. More than once when Alma was gone on one of her trips he'd drop by unannounced, or invite me over. At first, I gave him the benefit of a doubt—I thought, well, he's just trying to be friendly, or act like an older brother—but soon it became clear it wasn't a sister he was looking for."

I gazed at No. 4 in a way some might describe as provocative—simply to get my point across—but he just stared at me with a dumb expression on his face. I wondered whether he merely pretended to be dumb or whether he really was. Maybe I had to be more descriptive, I thought.

"Once, he invited me for dinner and, in my innocence, I showed up in blue jeans and a T-shirt only to find him all dressed up, waiting for me with candles and roses. Throughout the dinner I tried to convince myself that his intentions were honest, but when we finished, he walked up to the window and, taking in the dark sky, exclaimed, 'The moon is full tonight.' And then, he turned to face me—I had approached to look at the moon—and fixed his gaze on me: 'The way you stand now, wrapped in moonlight, you are like a golden goblet brimming with sensuous mystery.'"

I watched No. 4 to see his reaction, but he was taking everything in as if he were a spectator and I an actress on stage. He didn't ask, indignant, "What?!" but instead, looked on with wide-open eyes, as if he didn't want to miss anything. So, I went on:

"I was paralyzed. I couldn't even get away because his body blocked my passage. He moved closer, took my right hand in his hands, and with his eyes locked on mine, whispered, 'Your eyes seem full of goldfish swimming in a green pond. It makes me want to drown in them.' Of course, I shook my hand free and told him that his behavior was inappropriate; that he should have more consideration for my sister, and that, if this happens again, I'll let my sister know. Well, you wouldn't believe it … When he heard this, he stiffened, and his eyes grew cold, as if, from an appetizing morsel, I had turned into uninviting leftovers.

"The next time I saw the Architect he was holding my sister's arm and pretended nothing had happened. You know, this is funny, his behavior reminds me of a character in a novel of mine, a doctor who appears to be madly in love with his wife—who is, by the way, fifteen years younger—but, little by little, the reader realizes that the appearances are deceiving and his mad love is all pretense and phoniness meant to disguise his true intentions: to kill her. And, since he is a doctor, he chooses the method best suited for his profession: drugs. Once I understood that the Architect is my doctor's equivalent, the only thing to determine was what murder weapon an architect would choose. For months I couldn't come up with anything, until Alma gave me the key. She told me a story, a myth from the Balkans in which a craftsman who builds a cathedral or a church, I'm not sure which, for his king, has a dream ..."

Here, No. 4 interrupted me again, saying that he already knew the story.

"Oh, is that so? From whom? The Architect?"

He acknowledged that, indeed, he knew the story from the Architect.

"Well, in that case you know how it ends."

"Yes, it ends with the death of the mason."

"Is he a mason? I thought he was a craftsman. Anyhow, I didn't mean the death of the craftsman, that's not essential here. I'm talking about the immuring of his wife, and his belief that in order for a creation to endure, the creator needs to sacrifice what he holds dearest."

"I don't think Alma was *that* dear to the Architect,"

"That's precisely my point! *He would be able to kill her!*"

"I'm afraid that's not too logical."

"What do you mean? It's perfectly logical."

"I mean it doesn't match the logic of the story."

"Oh, it's more than logical. It's insane, but perfectly logical. I've been thinking about this ever since her disappearance, but I didn't dare believe it. But now, now that I've said it out loud, I know it's true."

"It seems to me that this is magical thinking. You are convincing yourself that it is true because it sounds true."

"What 'magical thinking'? What are you talking about? Look, whose side are you on? Maybe there is still time, maybe he hasn't gone forward with his crazy plans, maybe he's hiding her somewhere, waiting for a great project."

At this No. 4 began to laugh heartily, as if I'd made a great joke.

"You think this is funny! Frankly, I'm beginning to wonder … No, never mind. You know, I'm very tired, I'd like to rest, and besides, there is nothing more I could tell you."

That made him stop right away, as if a spring had broken inside his laughing mechanism. Who said that laughter is "something mechanical superimposed onto a living thing"? It must have been some French guy, because Patrice used to quote him all the time. Apparently, he was right. No. 4's face now lacked any sign of laughter, and his body adopted the deceptively meek posture of an itinerant salesman begging you to let him in as you are trying to shut the door in his face.

"Please, please, go on," he said.

"OK, OK, if you insist. What else would you like to hear?"

"Tell me more about the tent…."

"I told you all there is to know about it. It's because of the associations she has with that tent that Alma only feels safe inside such a space, which for most people would probably trigger anxiety. You know what I think? I think for her the French monasteries were like a big tent. But the Japanese temples—*that,* I don't know. I've never been in a temple. It's the

Architect, with his interest in Japanese architecture, who gave her a taste for them. In one of the postcards Alma sent me she said something about a space whose outward aesthetics and inward peace were an uninterrupted continuum. There was this letter she sent from Ninna-ji I still remember, because she tried to imitate my style, which she's always made fun of, calling it 'a concoction of rainbow-sorbet metaphors for the usage of the emancipated housewife.' In fact, the whole letter was written in what she called the style of Frau Nora, her name for me when she was in her mocking mood. I have it here somewhere, yes, here it is...."

You'd love the morning mist enveloping the garden in a shroud of dewy silence. (I'm sure I've seen this "dewy silence" in one of your novels; if not, you have my permission to use it.) The predawn winter pale light diluted with the foliage's liquid glimmer lends a watercolor quality to the entire landscape (Yes, I did wake up at six a.m. a few times to attend the early meditation.) Later, when the sun will have grown in the sky, and the dew will have evaporated, the whole garden will become a labyrinth of crisp brown and green lines with a few undulating interstices here and there. I was told that the most common trees, besides the maple, with its crown of fire, are the Chinese black pine, which is indeed very dark, and the Japanese fern palm. But I'm still unable to identify those "typical" Japanese trees with their contorted branches that seem to follow a crazy artist's perverse imagination—and, in fact, it appears that those trees don't naturally grow like that; their branches are forced to shift in certain predesigned directions, following the wooden poles and the ropes installed for this purpose. Isn't it strange how this twisted, tortuous version of nature, this artifice attempting to fool us into taking for natural something that is, in fact, artificial, has such a peaceful effect upon us? A monk I think I already told you about—a very young monk with a smile that would undermine the determination of the most self-possessed nun—explained to me that this peaceful effect comes from the intermingling of four different elements: sky (air), earth, water and sun (fire). He explained this as we listened to the rush of cold water, a rivulet descending a steep, zigzagging slope amid shrubs and boulders on the northeastern side of the garden.

"And yet, everybody believes that peace comes from silence. You, on the other hand, seem to be stating the opposite when you list the sound of running water among its necessary elements."

"*Natural* running water. What I am saying is that peace comes from silence, but silence interrupted by occasional sounds in nature: the gurgling of a river; a bird's chirping; the sound of rain."

"Oh, you mean sounds that produce a certain rhythm. Are all the four elements always necessary to attain peace?"

"No, not always. As long as the elements are in harmony. That's what counts. For instance, there are some gardens that don't have water in them—dry gardens, we call them. But even those have a dry river, that is, a meandering river bed of stones and pebbles."

"You mean that even in a dry garden water isn't absent; rather, it is present through the trace of its absence."

Here, the young monk looked at me, a little lost:

"Well, I'm not sure that's what I mean, but I think you get the idea."

As always when he was slightly embarrassed, he giggled and blushed like a virgin. Then, he added:

"You are a very good student."

Actually, what he said was, "You very good student." He tends to swallow indefinite articles and some verb forms, though his vocabulary is quite developed. Watching him under that bush with pink blossoms, his cheeks also a light pink, I thought that he was a teacher's dream student. One felt like ordering him, "Repeat after me!" or asking him the kind of inappropriate questions one can only ask in a language class: "What did you do this morning after you woke up?" And then, when the shy student dared to come up with his timid answer, one felt compelled to reassure him that everything was OK with a slowly drawn caress over his flushed cheeks or an even slower kiss on his innocent lips.

Yes, I felt an aesthetic impulse to be this monk's teacher, to watch over his diligent struggle with English phonetics, so the next day, when, following our now established custom, he offered me tea during my siesta in the lobby, I nonchalantly proposed that we practice English conversation every day "for at least two hours." At first, he seemed taken aback and, in his usual manner, he repeated my words, adding a question mark, "Two hours?" But he also produced some of those sounds I was familiar with from watching (at our Transylvanian relatives' persistent recommendation) some episodes of the 1970s Japanese animated TV series *Heidi*—sounds meant to express amazement, or wonder, or simply polite hesitation, and which invariably reminded me of a cute Japanese girl lost in the Alps, whose black, round eyes filled the screen, as her mouth opened wide to let out an aaaaah or a soooooo—or so it seemed to me at the time.

We started our English conversation class then and there, and he proved to be a very diligent student. As for his progress, more details later.

Alma

I asked No. 4 if Alma had mentioned the young monk to him, but he got flustered and mumbled that he couldn't remember. Ha! He couldn't remember! What man can't remember a potential rival?

"He is the one who invited her to spend time at Ninna-ji when she was having doubts about marrying you."

There! Now I got his full attention. Didn't ask any question, though, just stared at me in silence.

"Well, yes, she was having doubts—not about you, but about marrying again. It's not that surprising, considering her history.... And that's where she went, but apparently not for long, because she left the *shukubo* about a month ago. The young monk confirmed that she was planning to return to the States, as she'd told me herself. And this is where the thread breaks. We don't know if she ever returned, and if she did, where is she?"

I watched him, curious to see his reaction. His agitation had subsided, and he was now staring ahead with a sad, melancholic look. That was not the reaction I expected, and I got a little angry with him. I didn't want to be left alone to worry about Alma. It was his duty to worry together with me.

"I can't help suspecting the worst," I said. "My instinct tells me that the Architect knows more than he lets on. Think of it: there are only three people she could have gone to, since she has no place of her own: me, you, or the Architect. And if she went back to him, you can be sure we won't get anything out of that … that big bag of fat with aristocratic airs. But … maybe … maybe Patrice knows something."

I looked at him, but he just sat there with the same dumbfounded air, as if he'd never heard of Patrice.

"Patrice—the French Monk's sister. You absolutely have to talk to Patrice! There was a time when she and the Architect were quite close—closer than they should have been. When Alma first told me that there was something going on between the two of them, I thought it was her imagination, but now I know she was right."

I stopped, waiting for his question, which never came, so I asked it myself:

"Do you know why? Because meanwhile I myself had witnessed the Architect's wayward ways, so to speak. Didn't he try to seduce me too?

"Patrice really has a weakness for this man. That means, of course, that she may not be willing to tell you the truth; on the other hand, if she is jealous enough, she might. Take my advice: go and talk to Patrice! If there is anyone who knows anything, it's her. I told you everything I know."

He suddenly seemed to awaken from his absence, and asked if I happened to have another letter sent by Alma from Ninna-ji.

"I only have a short email announcing that she'd be back shortly."

"No, I mean from her previous trip there."

"Yes, I think I might have another letter ... let's see ... It must be in the same box unless I misplaced it.

"Here it is! It's a short one."

I've become so sentimental I'm afraid by the end of this trip I might turn into you. You should see me with my young monk walking under the maple trees, admiring the leaves' shapes and fall colors, listening with one ear to the birds' chirping and, with the other, to the monk's perorations. Speaking of bifurcated listening, could you use one of your ears to determine what Patrice is up to these days? Is she still sniffing around my house, waiting for the right moment to jump in the boat? Is she trying to alleviate a lonely man's solitude and kill two birds with one stone by also taking revenge on the woman who had "wronged" her beloved brother? Come to think of it, maybe you could help by stopping by some day and seeing what my husband is up to. And Patrice too. Briefly, see what both of them are up to!

"I was in no mood to pay a visit to either Patrice or the Architect, and see what they were up to, so I didn't. But dear life—or should I say fate?—has a way of setting things up for us. But first, please excuse me, I've gotten really thirsty, what with all this talk. Maybe you'd like a glass of water, too."

He drank the entire glass in one gulp as if all this time it had been him talking, then asked for another. When I came back I couldn't remember where we were.

"Where was I?"

"Fate."

"Oh, fate. Do you believe in fate? Of course not. You people in academia believe only in ... What is it that you believe in? Never mind. There is no doubt in my mind that that winter day when, on an impulse, I entered an old movie theater midday—something I never do because I only watch movies at night (as Alma says, watching a movie when there is still light outside is an act of both moral and aesthetic indecency)—to watch a black-and-white film from the forties, there is no doubt in my mind that on that day I acted under the demonic or divine spell of a force from above. Otherwise, what could have been the odds of my running into ... Oh, but speaking of a force from above, I just remembered my very first exchange with Patrice. I have to tell you this story!"

I told No. 4 how many years ago, when Alma was still married to the Monk, Patrice and I had been invited as the only guests to celebrate Alma's birthday. Somehow, the conversation turned to the subject of faith and God and, not without provocation (and also because I'd been warned by Alma), I turned to face Patrice and said:

"But you, like a true Frenchwoman, surely don't believe in God!"

She measured me with such cold, dispassionate spite that I felt she would have liked to use me as a handkerchief to blow her nose, or as a rag to wipe off her shoes. She then moved her gaze to her plate, and only then answered, without looking me in the eye, as if I was not worth the bother:

"My dear, the only thing I believe in is grammar."

She uttered this with such a dry tone it made me wonder how her tongue hadn't dried up inside her mouth, and with the most exaggerated French accent I'd ever come across: "My deerr, dee onlee ..." Hard to believe as this may be, this was her true accent.

No. 4 didn't seem to care much about my story.

"Can we go back to the movie theater?" he inquired.

"What movie theater? Oh, yes … Yes, the movie theater. It was a winter day with a bright, clear sky. I stepped out of the house, and my eyes were instantly blinded by—if you allow me to quote myself—'the scathing nudity of the sky, its shamelessness in uncovering itself before our naked eyes, teasing them with a cosmic striptease.' Yes, it's from one of my novels and it defines perfectly the sky on that winter day. Its brightness was almost intoxicating. I remember feeling light-headed and walking aimlessly until I happened upon that theater. A black-and-white photograph of Barbara Stanwyck was smiling at me in a devious way, as if inviting me to probe and see what hid behind those glowing, bare shoulders and those enormous, calculatedly cold-hearted eyes. Without giving myself time to think, I bought a ticket and entered the hall and, then, through an opening in a heavy burgundy velour curtain, the dark theater.

"There were only a handful of people inside: a very old woman in the front row; two teenagers a little further back, frolicking and kissing in a shameless way; and another, older couple, toward the rear. Cautious, I took a seat in the last row. But then, I don't know why, I decided to move two rows down, and I ended up behind the older couple. It was really an irrational move, since there were so many empty seats around. The movie started, and for about half of it I was entirely caught in its gothic atmosphere and twisted plot; but then the plot got more and more implausible, until it became so ridiculous that I started to look around, bored, and I noticed that the couple in front of me wasn't watching the movie, either. The man's right arm was around the woman's shoulders, and his face, slightly turned toward her, sported a thick beard. There was something familiar about his profile, but I just couldn't put my finger on it. The woman's shoulders were large, like a man's, and her dark hair was cut very short. The man began to playfully kiss the woman's ear, and she protested—well, sort of—giggling, 'Stop dat! You are teeckling mee!'

"I could have recognized that accent in a thousand. *Jesus*, I thought. When the next scene brought some more light into the room, there was no doubt: the man was the Architect, and the woman was Patrice. I was so shocked by my discovery that for a few seconds I could barely breathe. Then, I panicked. I had to get out of there without being seen. And so, five minutes before the credits, I stood up and sneaked out, my stomach tight as a ping-pong ball. I stepped out into the blinding light and began to run home, followed by the sky's mocking nudity.

"I can see that you too are shocked. You are probably wondering, well, if Patrice and the Architect are, or were, an item, what makes you think she'd tell you anything about him? And the answer to that is: revenge and jealousy. Patrice had her eyes on him for years, and she was very hurt when he married Alma. Then, she was hurt again when, after his divorce from Alma, he refused to move in with her, never mind marry her. If you ask me, Patrice tried to separate the Architect and Alma from the beginning. She was fooled by his double game; he led her to believe she had a chance, when in fact, all he wanted was to have some fun, and when Alma and the Architect finally split, Patrice was shocked to realize that reaching her goal was as improbable as ever. By now she must be filled with purple wrath, and when one is like that, one is likely to spill a lot of beans."

I paused to draw a deep breath in, waiting for his comment.

"Did you tell Alma about this?" he asked.

The question caught me unprepared, so I stammered:

"Tell Alma? Not right away, no … I was afraid of what she might do. But, eventually, I … yes … though I'm not entirely sure. At any rate, Alma knew."

The truth is, I couldn't remember at what point I *did* tell Alma. And, honestly, I'm not even sure I told her, strictly speaking, or if she just drew it out of me in one of our heated conversations when she was staying with me after her breakdown. Anyhow, it wasn't something I wanted to dwell on now, so I hastened to add:

"What is certain is that Patrice has had a thing for the Architect ever since she set eyes on him for the first time. I remember another dinner with her, this one shortly after my sister and the Architect got married. Patrice was staring at him as if someone had cast a spell on her, without even realizing how visible and obvious that was to all of us. Frankly, it was strange and off-putting to see such a physically strong woman, who was otherwise so blunt and unsentimental, blush like a schoolgirl at the Architect's most trivial remark, and melt like a maid when the Master addressed her. And the Architect! What an actor! What a devious Don Juan! How he pretended to have eyes only for his new bride when he was busily using his nose—and what a nose!—to secretly sniff the other two women at the table. Oh, I'd detected his hyenalike snout ever since I met him.

"When Alma walked out of the dining room that evening, I had the clear, unmistakable feeling that I was the fifth wheel, and that Patrice and the Architect were waiting for me to get the hell out of there so they could carry on with their secret and shameless conduct. And so, though I was dying to find out more, I followed Alma into the kitchen, but she ordered me to 'get back in there,' so I did, and when they saw me, they both looked startled, as if caught in the middle of something. They were standing next to each other by the bookshelves, and the Architect tried to hide his embarrassment by grabbing a random book, which happened to be one of Alma's French books, something about a saint with the name Léonie in the title. The Architect browsed the book absentmindedly for a few seconds, and then, looking at the title, said:

"'Funny, the name *Leon* spelled backwards is *Noël*. Christmas!'

"As he uttered the word 'Christmas,' the Architect looked Patrice straight in the eye, as if wanting to communicate a message I wasn't supposed to understand.

"'Speaking of Christmas,' I said, 'I assume Alma told you that I invited you two to my place.'

"'Yes,' he said, 'I think she mentioned something, but I'm afraid I won't be able to come, because I'm on a deadline and need to finish a project.'

"Before he'd even opened his mouth I knew exactly what he was going to say. And I knew it was a lie, and that the lie was connected to whatever happened in that room before I walked back in. But the funny thing is that soon afterward the book disappeared from the shelf. After Alma came to live with me, she told me that once, when she visited Patrice, she found that book in her library. It was a bewildering discovery, considering that it was the kind of book no one—Patrice least of all— would have any interest in reading. I really can't recall what it was about and how Alma came to possess it, but she told me that seeing it on Patrice's bookshelf gave her the uncanny feeling one would have if one found an intimate personal object, say, one's glasses, lost long ago in one of those moments of distraction when an object we are constantly in contact with suddenly and unexpectedly vanishes without a trace, and then, months later, we end up finding it in a place never anticipated. At any rate, it was one of those unexplainable things...."

As my gaze fell on No. 4, I saw that his eyes were closed, and his body was spread on the couch like that of someone who had fallen asleep. For a second I didn't know whether I should get mad or laugh.

"I see my stories are putting you to sleep."

He started:

"Oh, no, no, quite the contrary. It's just that I'm very tired. I haven't had a good night's sleep in weeks. But I'm very interested in everything you're saying. Please tell me more about your family. Alma never told me anything about them, and maybe there is something there, something to give me a clue...."

"If she didn't talk much about our family, she probably didn't mention our Hungarian aunt, Susana, or our trip to Budapest one summer when she was still married to No. 1."

And so I told him about our trip, and in doing so I found that it gave me great pleasure to *tell* the story, as much as writing novels does. The Berlin Wall hadn't fallen yet, but Hungary had started to move closer to the West and adopt a free market economy since the early seventies, and by the late eighties, when we were there, some freedom of speech was allowed, and life as a whole was less gray than in the neighboring countries. It was the first time that we, Alma and I, went abroad together, and the first time we went to visit our father's relatives. We'd been talking about taking this trip since we were kids, but the more we talked about it, the more it turned into an intangible, faraway project, until the summer Alma confided in me that her marriage was on the rocks, and I said jokingly that she should see a psychic, and she answered, yes, Aunt Susana, because—and you certainly don't know this—Aunt Susana is clairvoyant. She even has an office—if a table in her partner's bistro can count as an office.

This is how a joke took us to Budapest one summer day in the late eighties.

At first sight the bistro looked more like a pub, with its stairs descending into a cavelike, small room with walls of stone. The whitewashed, slanted ceiling was crossed by a heavy beam from which hung pots of red carnations, and the few tables were all of lacquered wood with high stools. The menu and the drinks list were written in chalk on blackboards, and a red-cheeked, plump fellow in his early forties presided over the place behind a counter with a green sign labeled *"Gösser."* Aunt Susana greeted him and introduced us with a long preamble, a preamble we didn't understand, it being in Hungarian, but we did understand that it was about us, her American nieces, her brother's daughters who didn't speak Hungarian and were visiting Budapest for the first time. The man let out an interjection of surprise, as did other people we would later meet during our trip, which at the time I interpreted as a sign of enthusiasm for the distant land we came from, when in fact it was merely a token of appreciation for our aunt. She was in her mid-fifties and, like most people in that part of the world, showed it: slightly plump, her posture verging on a caricature of femaleness, her round, overstretched behind threatening her balance but kept in check by her equally well-defined breasts. Unlike her brother, she was blond, the two of them thus creating a parallel couple to Alma and me. Her skin was tanned, with wrinkles around the nose and the eyes, and she didn't wear makeup, save for the very pink lipstick applied to her thread-thin lips in the clumsy way a teenager might have done. She always wore blouses with deep-cut cleavages, and crocheted skirts that accentuated her behind—this on top of her already very conspicuous figure—and she swung her hips in a way I've only seen done by African women or by chocolate-skinned women from remote islands. So, when she walked, all the male heads around us turned to follow her, a large smile on their senile faces. (Older men especially seemed fond of Aunt Susana.) She appeared to get a lot of pleasure out of this street show she performed each time she walked out of the door, and in fact, during the year she visited us, there was a man … Well, but I'm getting carried away—let's get back to the restaurant in Budapest.

We seated ourselves at one of the tables, and a minute later in came Gyuri, Aunt Susana's male companion, a man with the potbelly of a very pregnant woman resting on top of two skinny legs and two feet shod in plastic slippers. His entire being, starting with his drooping face, seemed to be pulled toward the ground by a gravitational force that acted stronger for him than for the rest of us. He hugged us, trying not to spill on us the ash of his lit cigarette, and then ordered pálinka all around. Aunt Susana also lit a cigarette. When Alma and I declined to help ourselves to her pack of Marlboros, she smiled snidely, and turned toward her companion to make a comment about Americans and cigarettes, which we didn't understand. Gyuri left soon afterward, and Aunt Susana switched to English, which she spoke almost fluently, albeit with a very strong accent, those Hungarian *o*'s pronounced the way one says *chalk*. She'd learned English when she lived in the States, yes, Aunt Susana had come to visit us when we were little, and at Father's insistence, she stayed for a whole year even though she hated it and eventually went back. From that period, Alma and I have gathered an impressive collection of hilarious memories we helped ourselves to whenever we were at a party and the conversation was slow, for "the adventures of Aunt Susana in America" were always sure to provide entertainment to a crowd of ironic hipsters. Of course, Aunt Susana had her own version of that visit, and now we were provided with it for the first time, because she didn't waste any time and launched immediately into her own memories of that year some seventeen years earlier. The last time she'd seen us we were still wearing diapers, she said, though it was probably true only of me, not of Alma. "You were both cute as a button, you more than Alma but she smarter than you," she added with the bluntness people have there.

And so she began reminiscing about her year in America—a place, she soon realized, she had no need for, no thank you. She punctuated her remark with exactly the same gesture of two decades ago, a gesture that fascinated us so: raising her cigarette very slowly, her hand in that pose of relaxed boredom and her head tilted to one side, a pose one sees in photos of Marlene Dietrich; and then, as she put the cigarette in her puckered mouth, drawing on it as deeply as she could with ecstatically closed eyes; and finally, after keeping the smoke in for what seemed like an eternity, letting it out in incredibly small rings for which Alma and I used to fight, placing our fingers inside as within a tiny Frisbee disc.

Now, here we were again, watching Aunt Susana almost as avidly, and wondering—at least, I was—where the calmness inside her came from. When we were kids, we (Alma more than me, as I was too little to initiate anything) liked to invent little torments for her because we got a kick out of her hilarious reactions—those *Iesus Mária*'s of hers spoken with childish indignation: childish because she never was angry with us, but rather ... perplexed at our unlimited inventiveness. Now, she reminded us of our past mischief as if she were still trying to recover from it, with one hand over her heart, like the Jewish lady on *Saturday Night Live*. No, we didn't do anything too bad, just kid stuff, like telling her that the salt shaker was filled with sugar, or that Americans like to put a dark red paste called ketchup on their desserts and encouraging her to do the same.

For months after she left, Alma and I kept repeating *Iesus Mária!* with our hands united in prayer and our eyes rolled up in despair, and then crossed ourselves quickly, as she did—and this silly theater amused us more than any TV show, sending waves of uncontrollable laughter through our tiny bodies.

Of course Aunt Susana asked us about Feri. At the time, Feri was a forty-something-year-old unglamorous fellow who had come to the States a decade earlier, and having unsuccessfully searched for a Hungarian woman, had ended up marrying "an American American," as he used to say. Aunt Susana met Feri when he came by one day to fix our kitchen garbage disposal and, charmed by his "perfect Hungarian" (which she contrasted with her brother's unpatriotic accent and mannerisms), by his twisted mustache, and hairy back showing generously when he crouched down under the sink, she forgave him for having married not only another woman, but a non-Hungarian at that, and embarked on a passionate affair that spanned the duration of her entire visit. Aunt Susana and Feri spoke on the phone for interminable hours—about what, we couldn't tell, because it was in Hungarian, though every now and then she tried to pronounce some English words we didn't understand, either, whispering them and making funny faces and blushing into the ear on the other end of the line. Whenever she attempted to speak English, Aunt Susana seemed to be holding a hard-boiled egg inside her mouth, and imitating her speech sent us into interminable fits of laughter. Although at that age we didn't hold the affair against her, we didn't appreciate her confiscating our phone line for hours at a stretch, and Alma, who was older and smarter, found a way to disconnect the phone while she was in the middle of some lovey-dovey confession. Every time this happened, Aunt Susana was just as surprised as the time before, shaking her head when Alma informed her that American phone connections were very bad. "And they claim that they are better than us," she muttered under her breath with all the spite she was capable of, enjoying once again the knowledge that American technology was, in the end, no better than its Hungarian counterpart.

"So, how is my dear Feri?" Aunt Susana asked, enveloped in a halo of smoke so thick that she looked like a genie who'd just emerged from a bottle.

"Well, Feri isn't getting any younger, but guess what? He got divorced two years ago."

"I knew it!"

"You knew it?"

"The cards!" Aunt Susana declared enigmatically, pointing at the pack resting on the table. "It's all in the cards."

"Oh … So, then, if you knew, you must have been in touch with him.…"

"Noooo … I haven't heard from him in ages.…"

"He isn't doing very well, you know."

As we explained to Aunt Susana that the amount of alcohol swallowed over the years was finally taking a toll on Feri's liver, she began to shuffle the cards, the cigarette still in her mouth, the ash suspended at its end in a precarious balancing act. The cards were like no other cards we'd seen before, with royal figures in red and green garments representing royalty from the Austro-Hungarian Empire—"Hungarian cards," Aunt Susana explained. The ash at the end of her cigarette was now half an inch long, ready to drop at any moment, yet continuing to stay there, in the air, in a way that defied physical laws and made it hard for us to focus on the cards. I know Alma must have been really irked by the ash—I could tell from the direction of her gaze and the fixed expression on her face. Finally, Aunt Susana took the cigarette out of her mouth with her right hand, while with her left she laid the cards on the table, and when we thought the ash was going to fall on the table, she aimed it at the porcelain ashtray without even looking at it, preoccupied as she was with the cards, and the ash fell effortlessly into the tray. Then, she drew again deeply on the cigarette, let it stay between her lips, and, thus freed, her hands returned to the colorful figures, which she moved with a magician's dexterity, right and left, left and right, now a king showing his mustached profile with a pointy hat, now a queen revealing wavy hair descending over round, silk-clad shoulders. She spread them in several rows, and, as each card presented its face to us, Aunt Susana's eyebrows moved up in silent dialogue with it. I don't know anything about cards, and being unfamiliar with the Hungarian images, I have no idea what meaning was attached to each of them. But I could tell that Aunt Susana wasn't happy with what she was seeing. She began to question Alma about her then-husband, No. 1: what he looked like, whether he had dark hair, whether he was violent, if he or his family came from a faraway place and if they spoke another language. She refused to elaborate or to explain those questions, she just said the cards were inconclusive; or rather, to use her words, "the cards refused to speak"—though they did allude to a dark man and a threat lurking in the future, so the best thing was to look for a professional, someone who was a star in the art of divination, and she knew just the right person.

And this is how we came to be acquainted with the Romanian Gypsy witch, Smaranda Biglip.

"Romanian Gypsies are the best in fortune telling," Aunt Susana declared firmly, "and Smaranda is in the top ten. People are waiting for weeks to get an appointment with her, so consider yourself lucky," she told Alma, who, I could tell, would have dropped the whole thing had I not given her one of my don't-even-think-about-it! looks.

"If you keep staring at me like that, I'll have to get a cure against the evil eye," Alma said dryly.

The truth is, I was curious to see a real witch. And yes, maybe my reasons were a little selfish, since even more than hearing what lay in Alma's future I was interested in having my own fortune told. And so it was that, barely three or four days after our arrival in Budapest, Aunt Susana took us to a rather sinister neighborhood at the edge of the city where dilapidated houses coexisted with barren plots of land on which lame dogs and blind cats strolled side by side in fraternal dejection. Smaranda's house was an imposing two-story building painted a painfully bright yellow on whose lower side white and light blue morning glories crept up with a dusty tiredness that stripped them of all their glory. There was a strange contrast between the size of the house, on the one hand, and the broken wooden fence surrounding it and the naked kids hanging around it, on the other.

Aunt Susana gave Smaranda the presents she had asked us to buy for her: a liter of pálinka and a pack of Marlboros. Judging from Smaranda's guttural voice, she must have been, like our aunt, an inveterate smoker. She appeared to be in her forties, though you never know with witches, and she looked very different from what I'd imagined. First of all, she was fat. Second, her face was banal in a disconcerting way: dark, with a few fine wrinkles, some prominent pimples—one never imagines a pimply witch; warts, yes, but pimples?—and unkempt, dirty hair. She didn't wear the traditional Gypsy clothing I'd seen on the streets, but a very casual blue dress whose hem was frayed. She invited us to sit down on the two wobbling chairs in the kitchen, and then went to the living room, returning with two upholstered chairs full of stains and smelling of urine. The house had barely any furniture in it, the walls were peeling off, and the floors, bare as they were, seemed covered because of the trash scattered all around—crumpled paper, apple cores, shells of pumpkin seeds, old receipts, broken toys, and other unidentifiable objects.

Smaranda didn't speak any English, but used an intricate mélange of Hungarian, Romanian, and Romani, so Aunt Susana performed the role of interpreter as best she could. As we waited for the coffee to boil, a grunt followed by a long, agonizing cough came from the adjacent room.

"My mother," said Smaranda, and invited us to meet the woman who, as it turned out, was also a famous witch, and whose name was—I'm not making this us up, I swear!—Baba Udder. Apparently, Baba Udder had been blessed with a pair of incredibly voluminous, tremulous breasts, whose aged remnants were still visible from under the blanket that covered her. Lying in bed, from where she displayed a face wrinkled like a sun-dried tomato, Baba Udder seemed a hundred-years-old, though in fact she was only in her seventies. A pungent smell of urine wafted from the bed, and both Alma and I kept our distance.

After we returned to the kitchen, Smaranda resumed the process of making the coffee, handling (explained our aunt) a Turkish pot in which the coffee had been boiled, and pouring it into some very small cups. Meanwhile, Baba Udder made her presence felt by kibitzing from the other room and ordering her daughter to let her see "the grounds." We understood what she meant once we finished drinking the coffee and Smaranda showed us how to place our cups face down onto the little plates. After a minute or two, during which time Smaranda and Aunt Susana succeeded in enveloping all of us in a cloud of Marlboro smoke, we each took our cup in our hands and examined it, making sure that all the liquid had been drained, and the configuration produced by the coffee grounds was stable. I had never imagined coffee grounds could generate such rich, mysterious worlds in which one could get lost, as in a labyrinth. I stared at the laced darkness in my cup as into a well, fascinated but incapable of making sense of it. It reminded me of the opaque, intricate beauty of Arabic calligraphy. Smaranda took Alma's cup and began to turn it this way and that, like a doctor examining an X-ray from all the angles. I whispered, afraid of disturbing her, that I'd never seen coffee made this way, and Aunt Susana translated my remark, laughing.

"Oh, it's Turkish coffee," Smaranda said, without interrupting her examination. "That's how we make it in Romania. The best one is done in the south of the country, where they make it in the sand. In the summer the sand gets so hot you can't even touch it." Then, turning toward Alma, and taking a toothpick in her hand, she added, "Let me show you your trip. See this long, long road here?" Alma nodded her head in acknowledgment. "That's the road you took to come here all the way across the ocean." As she said this, she scratched herself methodically under each breast, holding each of them with one hand, like a round, puffy loaf of bread, and using the other to perform the scratch. She wasn't wearing a bra, and the breasts—which had taken after her mother's—were moving freely, like (so I thought, making a mental note of it in order to use it later in one of my novels) "two wild animals."

"Let me see the girl's grounds, you harlot!" bellowed the mother from the other room.

"Shut up, you old *bolunda*!" the daughter quipped, but did go to the other room, and when she showed her the cup, the old *bolunda* let out a string of *Ay-ay-ay*'s, and the daughter asked, "Happy now? It's not quite *that* bad, what are you *ay-ay-aying* for?"

The old woman spat and answered, "It's death. That's bad enough for me."

That's the word Aunt Susana used in translation, *death*, and Alma and I looked at each other, then at Smaranda, as she returned with the fatidic cup. As she sat down to resume her investigation, she continued to question Alma, as if nothing had happened. Eventually, visibly curious but feigning nonchalance, Alma inquired, "What death was your mother talking about?" But Smaranda made a dismissive gesture, "Oh, this woman could see death just by looking into her asshole—pardon my language. I do see tears, though. See, here at the bottom of the cup. The bottom of the cup is your home. Tears, but no immediate death. But I see separation and fear of death in the future. You'll leave your man and travel to distant lands, and then you'll come back. But I can't tell you more, because the coffee grounds can only tell us about the present and the near future. I need to throw some beans and then see what the cards say." As she said this, she took a jar and spilled a handful of dry beans on the table, which she kept rearranging, furrowing her brow and muttering something. I saw Alma give Aunt Susana a nudge, curious, no doubt, to know what the Gypsy woman was muttering under her breath, but Aunt Susana pretended she didn't notice. The Gypsy woman kept muttering, eyes closed, her expression ever more focused, until she appeared to be in a trance, and then her voice grew louder, and the nonsensical words coming out of her mouth followed each other at increased speed, faster and faster, while her torso swung back and forth. Until then, I had been vaguely amused, but now I got scared. It's not that there was anything "evil" about the Gypsy woman; rather, there was something that reminded me of the irrational force of nature, something you don't think exists until you witness it.

The woman stayed in that state for at least three minutes, during which time none of us dared to even move. Eventually, she stopped swinging, and her muttering turned into a whisper.

When she stopped, she said, staring into the distance, but ostensibly addressing Alma, "You have a curse on you. And there are two men who'll come in your life, and both will build you a house, but it won't be a house of joy, it'll be a house of tears and regret. I see Death lurking behind the walls and behind the dark man."

"What dark man?" interrupted Alma.

But Smaranada just repeated her words, as if she hadn't heard her:

"I see Death lurking behind the walls of the house."

"Did you say something about a dark man?" insisted Alma.

Smaranda stared at her with empty eyes:

"You have a curse on you."

She now looked like a sphinx, and I wondered where the pimpled, fleshy woman she was half an hour ago had disappeared. Seeing that she couldn't get a straight answer, Alma went on, "And did you say that *both* men will build me a house? Do you mean a house from *each* of them?"

"I said *a* house from *both*," came the reply in an angry tone that cut off the possibility of any further questioning. Like the sphinx, the Gypsy woman expected us to figure out the riddle on our own. She got up, visibly annoyed, and turned toward our aunt:

"Is this girl simple-minded or what?" Then, facing me:

"And you, you need a man." She grabbed the cup from my hand, examined it for a few seconds, and then confirmed:

"A man! You need a man!"

I was dumbstruck because, indeed, I didn't have a boyfriend and was looking for one. After her double diagnosis, the Gypsy woman stepped out of the kitchen, and left us there wondering whether she'd be back or whether that was it. From the adjacent room, the intermittent and bellicose snoring of Baba Udder came in waves, and a dog kept barking nearby. We were getting ready to leave when, unexpectedly, Smaranda returned and handed Alma a small plastic jar, advising her to rub a smudge of the salve inside every night before bed on her forehead, her belly, and her breasts.

"It will undo the spell and lift the curse, but only if you use all of it. It's better not to use any of it than to start and not finish."

Alma took the jar with caution and held it two fingers away from her body, and in a tiny voice she inquired:

"May I ask what's in the salve?"

The witch measured her again as if she were dim-witted, and then began to list a number of things, which, translated into English by Aunt Susana, caused a burst of laughter from both Alma and me. We thought she was pulling our legs, but when we saw the look on her face, the laughter froze on our lips. The woman wasn't kidding. The salve was made of the fat of bear, dog, snake, and snail, combined with earthworm oil and crushed spiders. That's what she said! And then, turning to face me, she added, "And you, girl, do you really want a man?" I nodded: sure, I did.

"If you want to see your future betrothed's face, you shall step naked at midnight onto a dunghill, holding a piece of Christmas cake in your mouth." She paused, and inquired a little worried, "Do you have Christmas cakes in that America of yours?"

I swallowed, nervously: "Yes, we do, but I'm not sure we have dunghills."

She frowned: "You're *not sure* you have dunghills?! Well, if you can't find one, let me know and I'll ship you some from here. As I was saying, stand on a dunghill, and at exactly midnight listen for a dog's bark. From where the sound comes your future husband shall come. And now leave me alone! You've tired me enough."

We left, and as soon as we were back in the car, Alma exploded in uncontrollable laughter, while Aunt Susana shook her head and index finger the way she had when we were little and misbehaved.

"It's not a good omen to laugh at such things, dear girl."

As for myself, I was still befuddled, not knowing what to think or feel. Alma never used her salve, so for all I know she is still cursed. Years later, Smaranda moved back to Transylvania, where she was from, and when the Romanian government tried to implement a law penalizing Gypsies for false prophecy, she became a leader in the fight against it because, she said, "they should penalize the cards, not us!"

At this, No. 4 laughed, and then asked:

"So, did you stand on top of a dunghill, naked, with a Christmas cake in your mouth?"

"Ha! Ha! I'll let you wonder. All I can say is that, eventually, my betrothed did come, and then one day he left, and when he did leave, we were both barking like dogs."

"I think it's getting late …" No. 4 said, stretching and yawning. "Before I leave, could you tell me again how long ago Alma left the Ninna temple, and how the young Japanese monk confirmed to you her decision to return to the States?"

"A month ago, I told you. And the Japanese monk … well, by email, of course. I wrote him an email and he answered right back."

"Can I see it?"

"Sure—if I can find it…. Let's go to my office. This way … Yes, right here. It will only take a minute. Wait … There!"

Dear Ms. Nora, it is indeed a pleasure to hear from you.
I am confirming that your sister left our shukubo on

... and, to my knowledge, she returned to the United States. Please tell me when you hear from her.

P.S. When she left for the train station, she took a taxi with a man who comes here every year and with whom she was very friendly.

"I think I might know who this man is," No. 4 said unexpectedly.

At first, I thought I misunderstood, but he was clearly talking about the man from the taxi. It was my turn to bombard him with questions, except not in the patient way he'd been doing it:

"What do you mean?! You have to explain this!"

He explained that the Architect had shown him a letter sent by Alma from a previous stay at Ninna-ji, in which she mentioned a Japanese man traveling with his wife and his mother.

"I think it's the same man," he said.

"There is absolutely no guarantee that this is the same man! None! And even if it were him, they just took a taxi together, so what? Unless you think there is more to it ... No, I'm not suggesting anything, *you* are. Believe me, if there had been something going on between Alma and that man, she would have told me. She always tells me these things. If she didn't, it's because there wasn't anything to speak of. Which, come to think of it, is worse."

"What do you mean?"

"I mean, if she was having an affair with the man, it wouldn't be that bad—no offense. But the way things look, they just took a cab together, and then she disappeared. If he was the last man to have seen her, what conclusion can one draw?"

I hadn't even finished those words and I already regretted having said them. No. 4 dropped his head with his right hand over his eyes, as if he wanted to protect them from seeing what his mind was conjuring. Then, he raised his head toward the sky with both hands covering his eyes, as if imploring an invisible deity.

"Now, on second thought …" I said. "Why did the Architect show you that letter? I mean, why *that* specific letter? What was the point? Maybe he did it on purpose: maybe he wanted you to focus on this man, and thus avoid being himself the object of your focus."

At this, the poor man seemed utterly confused:

"I don't understand."

"He wanted to lead you in the wrong direction! Jesus! Isn't that clear?! I know it in my gut, in my heart, and in my mind: the Architect knows where Alma is! I know you don't believe me, and there's nothing I can do about that, but you should go talk to Patrice, and then you'll see that something is wrong, and that the Architect is at the crux of it.

"Do you remember the character Malcolm the Architect from my second novel? Oh, you haven't read any of my novels.… Well, you have plenty of time after you find Alma. In my novel I compare Malcolm the Architect to a spider, because the spider is the architect par excellence. And our architect, or rather, Alma's architect, or rather, Patrice's architect, is truly spiderlike. In fact, I don't know anyone who resembles a spider more than he does: ugly, hairy, with hideous tentacles ready to catch a harmless prey, skilled at weaving webs of deception and castles in the air. A spider dressed in an artist's mantle with a poisonous bite. I still don't get how Patrice, who has the head of a nuclear physicist, has let herself be fooled by him! But this is how we women are! Didn't *I* make a fool of myself a year ago with that crook of a cook? He was a cook in a restaurant, and, as it turned out, a crook. I can see from your eyes that Alma never told you the story. I'm beginning to wonder what in the world you guys talk about. He was like a Greek god: perfect body, and features as if chiseled in marble. I couldn't tire of looking at him; for four months I was completely insane. And yet everybody had warned me. If I had been an independent observer, and this had been happening to a friend of mine, I would have laughed at the poor idiot. Yes, a poor idiot, that's what I was until I realized that he'd been using my credit cards, and then one day he disappeared. I cried for two months, day and night; I thought I was going to die. Then, one morning I woke up, and the idiot that had lived inside me for half a year had vanished. Just like that! Isn't that the weirdest thing? That's why I understand Patrice—even the smartest woman can lose her mind every once in a while. But the problem is that in her case it's been years, and she still hasn't recovered. That's why she may be the best interlocutor you could find: she has a double perspective here, on the Architect's side *and* against him at the same time. Go and talk to her!"

Patrice

"I don't like to waste my time, and I don't want to waste yours, either, so I'll get straight to the point: I don't know where Alma is."

That's what I told him as soon as he entered my apartment, before he even sat down on the couch, after having attempted to sit on the handcrafted chair I'd brought all the way from Côte d'Ivoire, a very fine, one-of-a-kind piece, which I now luckily managed to save by letting out a powerful "Nooo! Not there!" Startled, he found refuge on the Ikea couch. I asked him to excuse the mess—at first, I couldn't remember the English word, so I said "*désordre*," which prompted an interrogative gaze, as if it was that hard to understand! After all, there is an almost identical word in English, but for some reason, Americans, even university professors like him, have a hard time committing to memory any word with more than two syllables.

I told him that if obtaining information about Alma's whereabouts was all he needed, there was nothing more I could add. If, on the other hand, he came to me for guidance, a good piece of advice was something I could always spare. "I see you are still young," I told him, "in one piece, with no limbs missing. Go find yourself another woman!" Yes, that's what I told him.

"If she doesn't want to be found, chances are her marriage plans have changed. It's that simple."

I had to calm him down, because he grew very agitated, saying that something must have happened to her, that she had probably been murdered.

"Oh, you Americans have such a gothic imagination! I doubt she's been murdered. Murder, big dramas, this is at the movies. Reality is always more prosaic. I'm sure at this very moment she's hiding in a hotel room in Tokyo or Paris, watching a murder mystery on TV."

Of course she could have called him, I agreed with him on that, but in the end, what for? To tell him the marriage was off? That's not so easy to do. And when one does it, one needs to offer a serious reason, and she may not have a serious reason. Had he thought of that? I mean that Alma is rather unstable, and she's been like that for over a year. How do I know this? Well, I've witnessed it myself, and it's hard to believe he dated her for several months without noticing anything. At some point she was convinced that her husband—I mean, the Architect— was trying to kill her. At first, it was poison. She thought he was poisoning her food and drinks. Once, when I was paying them a visit, he returned from the kitchen with two cups of coffee, one for her and one for me, and, as I was bringing the cup to my lips, she sprang up from her chair and took the cup away from me. Then, she gave me hers and ordered me to drink it. I drank it to the last drop under her insane gaze—truly a frightening gaze because it still kept some remnants of sanity in it while having at the same time the fascinating glaze (or is it "glare"?) of the mentally insane. Yes, glaze or glare, I am not sure which one it is, but they both sound appropriate because they come from another world, a world of self-multiplying distortions. When I finished the coffee, Alma, sporting a large smile on her face, turned to face the Architect and said, "Now, we're going to wait for her to croak." The Architect stood there, petrified, without a word. I wanted to get up and leave, but Alma grew hysterical and bellowed that she wished to see me twist in the throes of death. So, I sat there, and we all waited for me to croak. After two hours, she began to cry, then went to her room like a child whose dessert had been taken away.

But more terrifying than anything was her obsession that the Architect wanted to wall her up in one of his ongoing constructions, as in some legend from the Balkans she'd read about. Alma used to love visiting the various construction sites where the Architect worked, to literally poke her catlike nose—really, a small, slightly upturned, unintelligent nose—into his office, interrupt his work by placing a huge steak sandwich before him—a sight he couldn't resist—and, after watching him gobble it down (I had, in fact, said "gobble it out," but No. 4 generously corrected me. English prepositions still give me trouble), ask him to give her a tour of the premises.

One day—I don't recall for sure, but I think it was before her obsession with the poison—I asked Alma to accompany me to the Architect's office, because I wanted to talk to him about a friend of mine who needed an architect, and after reluctantly accepting, when we arrived there, she began to tremble, pointing to a white wall in the distance:

"See that? This is the end. This is how I'll end up: behind that wall."

I tried to joke:

"It's the end for all of us, my dear."

But she paid no attention to me, and just repeated her words, adding:

"Buried inside that wall."

At that moment she trembled so hard I could hear her teeth clattering.

"What are you talking about? And *who*'s going to bury you?" I asked whispering, afraid of what she might say.

She gave no answer, but grabbed my arm, still shivering, with the same pained expression on her face, and held me tightly. I patted her arm, and reassured her the way you'd do with a child that there was nothing to be afraid of. She was breathing with difficulty, and her distress wasn't diminishing, so I thought I could distract her by proposing to go see the Architect in his office. At that instant, her body stiffened, she let go of my arm, and, looking me straight in the eye, she asked, with a face warped by dread and anger:

"Are you with me or with *him*?"

I almost asked who *him* was, but then thought better of it. Of course I knew who *him* was. Again, I tried to take it lightly, giving a short laugh, and grabbing her arm again, I replied:

"Of course I'm with you."

But she shook her arm free and began to sob, or rather, to wail:

"*No one* is with me! I can't trust anyone."

That night, the Architect, after hearing my story, called Nora to tell her that her sister was in very bad shape and needed to see a doctor, but he couldn't take her, and wouldn't she be so kind as to do it? And so Nora arrived and took Alma with her, and this was the last time the Architect saw Alma until he was served the divorce papers. Like the ogre guarding the orchard with the golden apple tree, Nora stopped anyone from getting close to her sister, including the Architect, who was banned from seeing his own wife. I sincerely doubt Alma was seen by a doctor. Nora is one of those women for whom the peak of scientific knowledge lies in her chiropractor's *mumbo-gumbo*—I love this English expression!—and who think that if you eat a lot of fiber and organic veggies and have regular bowel movements, your mind will be "cleansed," too, as if your brain had the same structure as your intestines. I wouldn't be surprised if she tried to "cure" Alma with ginseng tea. I mean, this is the woman who went all the way to Budapest to see a witch that would help her find a man, and who, following the witch's advice, spent New Year's Eve naked, eating, at the stroke of midnight, a cake layered with dog fat. It may sound crazy, but I know this from the Architect, who knows it from Alma, who had accompanied Nora to Budapest. The cake was supposed to make her dream of her future betrothed, and dream she did, or so she claims.

I asked No. 4 if he had ever met Nora. It turned out that he'd had a long talk with her a few days before he came to see me. "I'm sure she told you some fabulous things about me," I said, laughing. I meant "fabulous" as in "fable," of course. The woman has quite an imagination!

"Have you read any of her novels?" I asked.

When he said no, I thought it was a good opportunity to instruct him on what he had missed.

"You have to! It's like taking a trip to estrogenland!"

As always when I get started about Nora's novels, it was hard to stop. Because when one mentions Nora one cannot help referring to American women in general. There is one thing I don't understand about American women: they often behave as if they tried to prove true the worst clichés about women, and then they complain that men "objectify" them by portraying them in that way. At the college where I teach, all the women read cheap romance novels, and then they complain that men don't take them seriously, or that these kinds of books are derided as "women's" novels.

"Well, have you ever seen a man read or write such a book?" I asked him, but he just stared at me, helpless, trying to guess what the correct answer was, as if I was setting him a trap. "I haven't," I continued. "At least, my male colleagues read a biography every now and then. Or else they don't read anything, but what's for sure is that they read less trash than the women."

And, God, it's not just what men and women read. Never in my life have I met a woman more defined by the very things she looks down upon than the American woman. The American woman is split in two by a fundamental contradiction: she is still a Puritan, but a Puritan who has read Simone de Beauvoir and has internalized the sixties. By "Puritan" I don't mean that she is sexually inhibited. No, I'm using the word in the sense we Europeans use it: a person who molds all her desires according to a model of "perfection" hammered into her brain all the way from Sunday school to today's advertisements. The Puritan woman wants to be the perfect wife, mother, and—in today's parlance—"career woman." No, I am not saying that Sunday school teaches women to get a career, of course not. What I am saying is that Protestantism is so pervasive in this society that it infiltrates every aspect of life, and that has nothing to do with "faith," though it has to do with *religion*, which comes from the Latin *religare*, *being tied* together. Thus, the contradiction and the split at the core of the American woman: deep down she is the wholesome wife from *The Dick Van Dyke Show*, but she feels obligated by the progressive values she's been taught in school, and especially by her idols, the French feminists, to look down upon what constitutes her very core. So, in the end, the American woman is a knot of tangled guilt and repressed desires, her sense of self oscillating between guilt at not performing her duties—both at home and at work—and the desire to transgress the oppressiveness of those very duties. Never in my life have I heard the word "guilt" as often as in this country. And because no one can live with such a sense of guilt, the only way for the American woman to make peace with herself is by finding a scapegoat: man and "patriarchal society." Man is guilty for the American woman's constant sense of inadequacy. The American woman is the greatest victim in the history of humanity. And guess what: the better off she is, the more of a victim she feels herself to be, because this is when her contradiction is at its fullest. Women who live in poverty, black women from the ghetto, are not torn between the desire to be perfect and the simultaneous wish to transgress this very desire. It is the woman from suburbia, the female professor spinning histories of transgressions while she herself hasn't left her prosaic chair since the nineteenth century, when she was doing embroidery on the same seat, who is the queen-of-all-victims. Only a woman through whose veins still flows the blood of despotic fathers of yore is so torn between the instinct to conform to everyone else's expectations and the poisoned resentfulness conformity brings with it.

I'm not entirely sure whether I told him all of the above or just part of it, but I concluded:

"We, the French, have an expression, "être bien dans sa peau"—to feel good in one's skin. Well, the American woman feels very bad inside her skin."

"Hmm …" he mumbled something I didn't understand. Then, louder: "I guess it depends on the skin."

Presumably he thought he was witty or something. But I couldn't be stopped, and he had no choice but to listen to my long-rehearsed ruminations about American society, which I periodically bring up with the Architect, him and no one else, as I doubt they would make me very popular:

"American society is, emotionally, morally and aesthetically, a male culture in that it holds acting and doing above anything else, in particular above suffering and feeling. Paradoxically, American feminists are the most responsible for the enshrinement of this culture by equating the 'emancipation' of women with their embracing of those activities that are traditionally done by men, and thus, by implicitly sanctioning these male values and allowing them to prevail. French culture, on the other hand, values passion—which, by the way, comes from the Latin *patire*, *passio*, which referred to the sufferings of Christ, and, by extension, came to mean suffering in general. Passion and suffering are for a French person, and for all the other descendants of the Roman Empire, interconnected: one feels by letting oneself be taken over, by not "being in control," as you Americans say. *To be patient* in the sense of waiting rather than acting, to be *a patient* who has been taken over by an illness and is in someone else's care, or to be overcome by *passion*— all these states have the same origin and represent a view of the world that is very un-American. Even our law recognizes in France the power of passion by giving a special dispensation to those who commit a crime of passion. The opposition between French and American culture is the opposition between a female and a male culture and aesthetics. A true feminism would be a feminism that embraces female values (passion, passivity, nonaction) as superior, and tries to change the nature of man, and not the other way around. It is no accident that Proust—the most French of all writers, who also happened to be gay—is a writer who exalted suffering, whether caused by love or illness, and transfigured it into a metaphysical condition. Americans are bent on eliminating suffering, which is, basically, the equivalent of wanting to eliminate the female nature in them."

No. 4 was silent for a good minute. Then, somewhat shyly, he coughed, and said:

"Yes, I see your point … or rather, points. But, to turn to our … our discussion, I am not sure I understand where you are going with … What I mean is that I am not sure whether when you speak of what you call 'the American woman' you are referring to Nora, or to Alma, or both, or either, in which case, I think we should go back to … Do you see what I … You see what I mean, don't you?"

"I see I need to be more clear. I was referring to some characteristics of the American woman as seen by someone who had the luck to be born in a different land; but, at the same time, as I already mentioned, I was referring to the woman we both know as Nora, who shares many of the above characteristics. Nora is the kind of woman for whom the man is always guilty, and I am convinced that she did her best to persuade Alma to get a divorce, and that, instead of taking her to a doctor, she very likely reinforced her paranoia. In fact, I wouldn't be surprised if Nora was at the origin of Alma's fantasies. In the end, all those Hollywood movies and paperback novels she's read could not have been without an influence on her already fragile brain.

"Those scary movies with dubious characters who, under the appearance of domestic normality, are hiding deviant desires and plotting killings, dismemberings, or who-knows-what—those movies made for the sole purpose of exorcising people's inner demons, the way children like to scare themselves by making up evil monsters hiding under their beds—could only have been created by a puritan society; a society obsessed with order and good behavior, in which passion is turned into its opposite: pathology. In this society, a housewife's Bovarian fantasies lose the purity of passion. In the American version of *Madame Bovary*, the housewife would have killed either her lover or her husband, not herself. What I am trying to get at is that Nora, although divorced, is the prototype of the American housewife, and that in her housewifely mind she has already condemned the Architect as her sister's killer."

"Don't you think you are a little—at least a little!—biased in your assessment of Nora?"

"*Biased*?! Am I *biased*?! Of course I'm biased—that's why I have a brain! Any judgment is biased by its nature. Only a vegetable is never biased. The question is not if we are biased, but if we are biased in the right direction. By the way, 'biased' comes from the French '*biais*,' which means *slanted*; that is, *inclined* in a certain direction. If you have no bias, that is, no inclination, you might as well have porridge inside your skull."

It was clear that the man knew more than he was letting on. That is, his question had been clearly "biased" in that it implied that I might have a reason not only to hate Nora but also to protect the Architect.

"Let's get something straight," I said. "I don't like to be taken for a fool. I know Nora told you that there is something going on between me and the Architect. And she's right, there is something going on, except not what she thinks."

I explained that I bought my brother's house—the one with the tower—and I was considering various changes and ways of improving it. The Architect was now working for me. He thinks I should let the tower be, rather than take it down, as I'd initially intended. Of course the loft will serve a totally different purpose. In fact, a few weeks ago I mentioned this to Alma, and she proposed something that at the time seemed totally silly but that eventually got me thinking: a "meditation room."

I've always believed that this vision of meditation that has been transplanted to the States and Western Europe by all those half-baked, self-proclaimed Indian gurus is a hoax, a fraudulent way of exploiting the Achilles' heel of a society defined by work and efficiency, and which, as a consequence, is eager to let itself be soothed into childish sleep by any crook who has learned the lesson of the West: praise the very things that stand in opposition to what people most believe in (work and efficiency), and they will follow you like sheep. But be careful to package it the only way they can understand it: meditation as a practice in a regulated environment with a sign around your neck to announce that you are "meditating."

Well, if I had a "meditation room," that very purpose would stop me from meditating. Still, ever since Alma proposed this, I couldn't help envisioning an empty room with a chair in the middle of it, so in the end, I think this is what the loft will look like. I even came up with a name for it: "the Room of Sacrificed Desires." When the Architect heard this, he grew very excited and said that it was the perfect name and purpose for his tower. A tower leading to a Room of Sacrificed Desires.

"When Alma got wind of it, she proposed—guess what? To cover the walls with magazine clippings of stories about sacrificed desires. Now, excuse me for repeating myself, but this is a typical American reaction! Over-representation. Typical materialist impulse. I'm using the word 'materialist' in its literal sense, from 'matter.' Love of matter."

"I'm afraid I don't understand."

Of course, you don't understand, you're an American, I thought but kept my mouth shut. I tried to explain:

"Most people, when thinking of 'sacrificed desires,' would think of a *lack* of something. Something that is not there. Unrepresented. But what does Alma, the American woman, propose? Well, she proposes an overabundance of things. 'Stuff,' as you Americans say. Clippings all over the walls. It doesn't cross her mind that the best way of representing sacrifice or lack is by not showing anything. An empty room with a chair waiting for someone."

As always when talking about these things, I got carried away. I shouldn't have called Alma "the American woman." At that instant I made an enemy of him. I could sense his enmity grow inside him like a taut bow, with the arrow waiting to spring forward and hit me. So, I tried to fix things by giving them a more theoretical polish. I told him about the novel I'd recently read by an early twentieth-century avantgarde Russian writer, Sigizmund Krzhizhanovsky, *The Letter Killers Club*. The "club" is a group of friends who decide to "kill" letters by turning storytelling into a process of virtual existence, and thus, reducing stories to abstractions that are never materialized.

"What I meant is that Alma is the opposite of a letter killer," I said. "She is a *letter birther*, and in that sense, a materialist."

"I think you don't know Alma at all!"

His explosion took me by surprise.

"You are using her as some kind of springboard to illustrate your own idiosyncrasies, but in fact you don't know her at all," he continued, agitated. "And besides, who *isn't* a letter birther, or whatever you want to call it?"

I felt I had crossed a line, and bit my tongue. And maybe he was a little right about the letter birther thing. So, I hastened to add that, yes, he was right, we were all materialists in that sense. In fact, I had decided to allow myself more than a little bit of materialism in the "Room of Sacrificed Desires" by covering the walls with a French tapestry and a Japanese silk scroll. After all, I am not a monk—or a nun. And maybe Alma's suggestion had less to do with materialism than with a fundamental difference between the ways the Americans and the French envision space. Americans are pioneers of space; they move ever more toward the periphery. Even when they reflect on things, they always start by defining their borders, like lawyers for whom nothing exists in itself but only through intercourse with other things they come in contact with. For an American, inhabiting a space means framing it. For a Frenchman, exactly the opposite: grounding yourself in the center, and from there, opening the exterior through concentric circles. When a Frenchman reflects on something, he begins by defining the origin of that thing; that is, the matrix, the center, where everything originates. By contrast, for an American, thinking means guarding the borders of a predetermined field. You can see these two different visions of space in the way American and French cities and villages are structured. In America, they are all rectangular; in France, all the villages and old towns have grown around a church or a cathedral, and if you look at them from a distance or a hilltop, you can see that they are round.

"Speaking of space," I added, trying to ease the tension a little, "I had just returned from the dentist before you arrived. That was a most curious use of bureaucratic space."

I told him how I'd thought I had accidentally stumbled into an Aldous Huxley museum. It was a building with numerous offices, all with their doors open, creating a sort of large playground on which, instead of playing, the children had their teeth pulled out; well, not exactly pulled out but, rather, straightened with braces and other similar devices. Colorful balloons descended from the ceiling; a fountain shaped like a big iron globe on which water delicately murmured decorated the middle of the waiting area; and a corner with some kind of plastic structure colored in purple, lime green, and pink was occupied by a toddler holding a yellow crayon and expressing his thrill at being there by tracing lines on a sheet of paper placed before him, right on the floor. A woman who was apparently the toddler's mother stood by the counter, engrossed in conversation with the receptionist.

The receptionist—of undefined age, maybe twenty-five, maybe thirty, maybe fifty—was dark blonde, with freckles that extended all the way to her low-cut neckline. She had a pen in her hand and a smile on her face, modulating both according to the rhythm of the conversation. Next to this receptionist was another one, also dark blonde, but without freckles and with a blouse whose collar followed closely the line of her neck. Since she wasn't talking to anyone, I went up to her, and she welcomed me with a smile identical to that of the previous receptionist. Although I am not prone to easy smiling, I can't let a smile go unanswered—it would seem like not answering a greeting—so I smiled. I thought that now that we had both smiled, we could get down to business and focus on my dental problems; but she kept smiling, so I had to smile, too, which prevented me from concentrating on my poor English, and as a consequence I spoke so inarticulately and with so many errors that I had to repeat myself, all the while keeping a smile on my face because she wouldn't abandon hers, so by the time I finished explaining my situation, my mouth hurt so badly I had an extra reason to be in a dentist's office. Eventually, we ended our painfully silly conversation, and she ushered me into a tiny room where another fair-haired woman of identically indeterminate age with an identical ethereal smile greeted me.

I sat down in the patient's chair with the radiant confidence that any seat or chair gives me, all the more so since this time I was protected by a blonde angel. The angel kept chirping and adjusting her smile to the changes in her intonation: if her voice went up, the corners of her mouth went up, too, and her eyes sparkled with joy; if her voice went down, the corners of her mouth went, of course, down, and, for a brief second, her face took on a sad expression. Whenever her mouth went up, her teeth showed—white and impeccable, as were the teeth of the other previous angels.

As I was getting ready to savor my chair-induced indulgence, a chorus of voices rose from outside, and I turned my head toward the open door: about seven to eight blond girls in white lab coats sang and clapped their hands, while a shy, dark teenage girl stood in their middle, smiling clumsily. But she too had nice teeth. "You can go home now/You are brace-free," sang the chorus, and I realized that they were celebrating the removal of the girl's braces. Then someone brought a cake—it looked like a carrot cake, but I couldn't be sure from where I was watching— and they began to cut it in pieces and distribute them. I felt I was witnessing an extraordinary, aboriginal ritual, and I wanted to take notes to be able to tell people "back home" about it, but I had no pen and paper; besides, I felt too comfortable in my cozy dentist chair, so I simply took mental notes.

"It's as if in this country everything is made for the children—the space, the food, the movies—or rather, as if the adults are treated like children," I concluded.

"Yes, we do love children," he replied.

What an idiot, I thought, but, afraid that he might have guessed my thoughts, I said, trying to sound conciliatory:

"Well, you are probably beginning to get frustrated with me."

He raised his eyebrows, defensively: "Oh, no, no …"

His nice-boy reassurance got on my nerves, so I quickly dropped the pacifying tone:

"Sooner or later, everybody does. You must think that I am but a frustrated middle-aged woman who can't stop complaining and criticizing everyone—isn't that so? Come on, admit it! I know quite a few men who claim that they are attracted to intelligent, powerful women, but what they mean by that is that they are attracted to women who find *them* intelligent. As soon as they sense that the women begin to see them for who they really are, the attraction is gone. This is because men—and, in fairness, women too—are attracted to the ideal image they've fashioned of themselves, which they hope to find in the eyes of their partner. Narcissism—this is what so-called 'love' is all about. This is why I can't find a man: no man can see in my eyes the beautiful lie he expects about himself."

Again, he opened his mouth and said exactly what I expected he would say:

"I can't believe you can't find a man smart enough to appreciate all you have to offer!"

This time I exploded:

"Please, don't patronize me! And don't feel obligated to compliment me! I hate flattery. Besides, I have nothing 'to offer.' There is nothing I hate more than mushy talk à la Oprah."

He then had an unexpected reaction. His spine seemed to strengthen, his face took a brave expression, and his voice was decisive and unfaltering when he opened his mouth:

"Glad we straightened this out. Now, let's get back to Alma!"

And so we went back to Alma.

Alma. When I first met her at Notre-Dame de Jouarre I never would have imagined that this pretty but otherwise insignificant young thing would play such a role in my brother's life and, indirectly, in mine too. I should have known that more often than not, major events in the lives of charismatic people are set in motion by marginal characters. My brother would have probably left the monastery anyhow—with or without Alma.

But what bothers me is that she never understood the chance life had given her. Yes, I am referring to her meeting my brother. Oh, yes, she "loved" him. Of course she "loved" him! What woman wouldn't love a man who looks better than Richard Burton and is more faithful than a saint? "Love"! I know what "love" means for women like her. It's all about the power to seduce. And then, when they reach my age and that power is gone, when the younger ones are playing the game they had played in their youth, all of a sudden they begin to scream that we live in a patriarchal society in which men control the game. Well, it didn't bother them before, did it?

That's the sentence I used, I remember clearly:

"Well, it didn't bother them before, did it?"

I remember it because in order to reach the proper English intonation I had to raise my eyebrows in a dramatic way, and as I kept them suspended like that, I saw his stern, unamused expression. We stared at each other like that for a few seconds, I with my clownish eyebrows, he with his widower's dejection. It struck me then that he was truly sad, and for the first time I felt sorry for him. I wanted to say something vaguely consoling, but the closest thing to sympathy I found was to reminisce about my brother's falling in love with Alma, and thus, by summoning a twin experience, to give No. 4 something hopeful he could hang on to:

"I remember the first letter I received from my brother that summer after I left him with Alma. He didn't mention her name, yet it was everywhere, creeping in between every vowel and consonant with a stubbornness I later realized belonged to the bearer of the name. 'Something has happened,' the letter began, 'something that has touched my soul with the power of a new beginning. It's as if someone has removed a veil that has hitherto covered my face whose raw flesh is now exposed to the world—a new soulface.' He then began to muse over his childhood, colored by his particularly strong affection for our mother, who was a curious mixture of rock and silk, solid and unbreakable, but also blessed with the gift of charming, something she did with her forget-me-not blue eyes (which my brother inherited) and a smile that captured the space between two perfectly symmetrical little dimples and two fine wrinkles on each side of her mouth. Yes, she was steady as a rock, but there was nothing brittle in her, she was smooth like a feline, or as silk—which she loved! She was the only person I've ever known who never made a clumsy gesture, which, of course, I found fascinating, I being such a klutz."

As I said the word "klutz," I wondered immediately whether it was the right word. It *sounded* right, like one of those words whose envelope is a perfect reflection of its meaning. Then, I felt ill at ease—why was I revealing all these things about my mother to a stranger? Delving into the past is like eating peanuts: one is never enough and it's always followed by another one and another one. I couldn't move away from the images of my mother during my summer visits to their house—so much more modest than the house my father and I lived in. I never got tired of staring at her, this beautiful stranger who was my mother. With her, everything was flow: the fork to her mouth and between her rounded lips; her white throat pulsing like that of a proud swan; her gaze, blue and limpid, to the window and back to us; her white hand, small yet elegant, on the glass, with her spread fingers, as if playing an instrument, then back to the table; her hand lifting the pack of cigarettes with the fingers arched down from the wrist like a dancer's.

It wasn't just me; it was my brother too. In fact, I dare say my brother was in love with our mother. For the first six years of his life he was virtually glued to her skirts. My image of him is of a little boy with the soft, moist, frightened gaze of a deer, putting his tiny arm around Mother's hips, or, when seated, hiding his face in her lap with his arm around her waist. Like most young boys, he used to say that when he grows up, he'd marry his mother, but in his case, "growing up" was quite traumatizing. One day, the neighbor's child told him, laughing, "Nobody marries his mom, you stupid! You go to Hell if you do!" My brother came home crying, and after our mother explained to him as best she could that when he grows up he *won't want* to marry her, and that all boys are happy to marry other women, he began to sob with even greater despair, stammering that he'd never marry anyone else. Ever. And he kept his promise for a long time.

I always wondered what it was about this girl, Alma, that made such a difference, why it was she who changed his course. Sure, she's attractive, but there have been other attractive young women at the monastery—true, not many. It's usually the dry, unsalted husk in her fifties, a principled high-school teacher concerned with "our education system," that tends to vacation there. It's not attractiveness that is at issue here. It's power. She does have a certain power or, rather, energy. I experienced it myself. Not the power that comes with goodness and a classical beauty, the kind of power women have in fairytales, and with which they subdue not only the people around them but also and equally the beasts and all of nature. No, hers is a selfish energy, like that of a vacuum cleaner. She doesn't radiate—the way some beautiful, powerful women do; she absorbs everything like a vacuum cleaner or a python. That's how she swallowed my brother, and he, poor thing, slipped inside, whole and naked, like a saint. Then, she spat him out. Yes, luckily for him, she spat him out before she digested him entirely, so there was still something left of him.

I knew, of course, that it would come to this. That's why, after our mother died, and my brother and Alma were already living in the States, I decided to move here myself. It wasn't easy; in fact, it may have been the hardest decision of my life, having to leave my teaching job in France and all the benefits that came with it. Well, but in the end it turned out all right, the teaching position I now have at this community college pays just as well. If it were only for the money, I could live here for the rest of my life, but God, how can one survive in this *désert spirituel*?

I'll never forget the first party I went to in this country, shortly after my being hired at the community college. I was still dizzy with the world around me, as if I were still suffering from jet lag; I lagged behind—a flying saucer in a foreign sky.

The party was on campus, and on the invitation was marked not only the time when the party was supposed to start (6 pm) but also the time it was supposed to end (7:30). I had never attended a party whose end was decided from the beginning. So, rather apprehensive, I entered the designated room: at first I thought I must have mistakenly entered the wrong place and come to a party for preschoolers with colored balloons attached to the chairs lined against the walls, and sparkling bottles of Coca-Cola and 7-Up placed on the table. No alcohol. No cigarettes. No food, just chips and cookies.

I realized I was in the right place when I recognized two of the secretaries from the languages department, both wearing those funny, pilgrimlike dresses. Buttoned all the way up to the neck, they were cheerfully revolving around the organizer, Patrick, awaiting his instructions. I had the feeling that there was something in this scene—a secret meaning, a mystery—that was withheld from me, and that the initiates (Patrick and his entourage) would eventually disclose it. They will eventually take out the bottles of wine hidden under the table and say,

"Surprise!" *Yes, that must be it*, I thought, suddenly thinking that Patrick's name itself was not only the masculine version of my own name but a cover for something else, a *trick* waiting to be revealed. There he is, preparing to tell us something.

There he was, in the middle of the room, from where, beaming with happiness, he announced that we would all play a game. A game! What was this, kindergarten? This must be another trick. He explained the rules: we would start seated on a chair, and then, when he clasped his hands, we would get up, mingle, and try to occupy another chair. The one left standing was out. I was paralyzed. I couldn't move my legs. Will the old Vietnamese ladies with parchment-wrinkled faces, who worked three jobs and very likely never played games, go for this? And the old Russian professor who always sported that severe, distant expression? I looked at them. With big smiles plastered on their faces, they were all fighting for their chairs. I was the only one standing. I was out.

The following game was something called "a raffle." We each wrote our name on a piece of paper, which we then folded and put it in a basket, from which Patrick randomly picked a name. With the piece of paper in his hand, he stared at me, his smile extending all the way up to his ears. "Congratulations!" he said. What was he congratulating me on? He put a potted plant in my hands and everybody applauded. I stood there, like a vegetable rooted to the floor, holding my green, potted sister.

That evening, at home, I kept staring at the plant. I was still confused, but out of the fog, a thread of clarity was beginning to emerge. I understood I was back in kindergarten and I had to play along.

As my mind was wandering, I heard No. 4's barely audible voice:

"Do you think she'll come back?"

He seemed to be begging for a hopeful answer, so I said: "Of course she'll come back." Then, feeling that I might have been a little too uncharacteristically optimistic and he might think I was patronizing, I added, "She will come back, all right. But whether she'll come back *to you*—that, I couldn't say. I guess it depends on … hmm … Let me ask you something: you said, when you came here, that you wanted to know the truth, whatever it might be. Are you sure you want the truth? Are you sure you wouldn't blame the messenger, as they say?"

He gave a vigorous nod of the head, so I continued:

"Very well, then, I'll tell you the truth. Keep in mind that the truth is always different from the appearance. The Architect suspected that Alma was having an affair with the young Japanese monk, and he was right in being suspicious, but wrong in identifying the target. It happens all the time with couples. One partner will notice some changes in the other and start … what's the word? Sniffing around. One usually gets suspicious when their partner is cheating on them, or at least, fooling around— funny expression, I should say. Not to mention the preposition. 'Around.' One does so many things *around* in English. But the irony is that one's suspicions are almost always directed toward someone who incarnates a rival-fantasy rather than the real-life rival. Once, when I was young, I was dating a man who had a complex because he was very short, and at some point he grew very jealous of a friend of his who was tall and also happened to be a doctor—which was what my boyfriend aspired to be. He was convinced I was cheating on him with his friend, and he was half right. I was indeed cheating on him, but not with his friend, whom, by the way, I found totally unattractive."

This is how I prepared No. 4 for what I was about to say. So, coming back to Alma, I told him that the Architect's suspicions were right, save for the fact that they were misdirected. At this, No. 4 gave me an inquisitive look. I know it from Alma, I explained.

"I didn't realize she was confiding in you," he commented with a frown.

"Normally, she didn't. But this was before she wanted to 'see me croak.' We were on friendlier terms then. Besides, I know she confided in me for one reason: she thought I was going to clue in the Architect, and she wanted to make him jealous. But she was wrong: I didn't tell him anything. I told no one—until now."

Before I told No. 4 the story, I asked him if he wanted to drink something, and he asked me for ... milk. "Milk is for children," I almost said, but, thankfully, managed to keep my mouth shut. *Americans!* I thought, and brought him a glass of milk. I felt sorry for him. He seemed so ... hopeless. He took the glass and placed it—and my heart skipped a beat for the second time that day—right on the teak table that had been shipped only months ago from Indonesia. I took the glass and set it on a coaster on the coffee table at his right.

"Where were we? Yes ... The secret man who wasn't the Japanese monk.

"It started when Alma was in the *shukubo* near Kyoto. That's how they met. At first, he was no more than a casual acquaintance, a rather elusive middle-aged man with nothing much going for himself except for his dark, melancholy look. I remember her remark about the deep violet circles under his eyes, which she found attractive. After she returned home she didn't even give him a thought until four months later, when he wrote her, letting her know that he was coming to Boston on a business trip, and wouldn't she like to meet him?"

"What kind of business?"

"Well, that's the thing, he was very elusive about that.

"When they met, she barely recognized him in his well-cut suit and with his confident gait, under the nocturnal light of a glitzy downtown bar. After he drank a string of four or more Bourbons on the rocks, he discovered a Steinway piano in a dark nook and, in the almost empty bar, improvised some popular American songs, 'My Funny Valentine' and the like. He was so different from the reserved, sickly looking man who shuffled his slippers through the *shukubo*'s halls that she began to wonder whether it was the same person. She asked him where he'd learned to play like that, but he just gave her a purposely enigmatic smile. He appeared to her like an outline drawn on the night's blackboard, half shadow, half quicksilver, so much in contrast with the previous man she'd met that he didn't have to work too hard at it. *It*—you know what I mean. Here I'll do what movies used to do in the past when lovers went to bed: just move on to a new scene. And this in spite of a rather immodest, if not altogether vulgar confession made to me by Alma about that night, which only confirms my suspicion that she was using me as a way of settling scores with her husband.

"You know she thought the two of us—the Architect and I, that is—were having an affair. Which was *not* true."

At this, No. 4 just made a gesture with his hands, as if to say that he was not responsible for what other people were thinking.

"I am telling you this for a very specific reason. Do you have brothers or sisters?"

"Yes," he said, a little surprised. "Two brothers and two sisters."

"Then you probably can't understand what it means to yearn for a sibling."

"But you have a sibling yourself."

"Yes, but we didn't grow up together. I only saw him on holidays, and besides, there is a big age gap between us, and when one is young, one needs someone the same age. When I met the Architect I felt as if I finally found the sibling I never had. Whenever we converse we are in complete agreement, finishing each other's sentences, like twins separated by the accident of geography."

I almost described to No. 4 the scene of our first encounter, but I stopped in time. I would have regretted it dearly, I'm sure. I keep forgetting that this man still is, at least in theory, Alma's fiancé. But as soon as I pulled back all those memories inside myself, I felt that their weight was an enormous burden, and, maybe because of that, I couldn't stop replaying them in my mind.

The first time I saw the Architect we were both guests at a dinner, he a friend of one of the hosts, who was also an architect, and I a colleague of the other host, a math teacher. The Architect took half the space of his side of the table, though he isn't quite that large. It's as if his personality spilled beyond the outline of his body, making him seem even larger. And when he spoke, his voice sounded so familiar—a strange feeling I'd never had before or since. It's as if I'd grown up with that voice, and then at some point it disappeared from my life without my noticing it, and now it was back again, and I felt I was returning to warmth and safety. It's hard to describe a voice, but his has a resonance that shuts away anything else, low yet clear, like the vibration of a cello string on a quiet Sunday afternoon.

Once this scene came to me, others followed, images I couldn't rid myself of. One, in particular. Of this one, I never talked to anyone. No one, including the Architect, will ever know what I felt that afternoon when he stopped by to tell me he was marrying Alma. As soon as he opened the door I knew something was terribly wrong. By a tacit agreement we had decided not to mention Alma's name after she'd left my brother and it became clear that she and the Architect were lovers. For a few weeks—the weeks when the two of them must have been in that brief period of carnal ecstasy that people pay so heavily for once it's over—he'd stopped seeing me. Then, as soon as Alma left my brother and moved in with him, he started coming by again, sometimes daily, even if only for a few minutes, as if he needed that time away from what was now banal domesticity. He was not the marrying kind. That's why I thought I should give him a few weeks with Alma until he "got it out of his system," as they say. Not in a hundred years would I have thought he'd marry her. He himself had told me many times that he had no wish to marry.

That afternoon there was something about him that made me step back and really look at him. A guilt that wrapped him like a cloak and made his dark face even darker, his beard and thick brows even bushier, his broad shoulders drooping under a heavy weight. I was so afraid of what he might say I hoped he'd never speak again. And for minutes he didn't say a word. He just sat on the rug with his back against the couch on which I was seated. Then, after a long time had passed, he turned toward me, buried his forehead between my knees, and talked in a low, muffled voice:

"Alma and I are getting married."

The sentence floated in the air and vanished there before I could grasp it and make sense of it. I wasn't sure of what he'd said, yet I couldn't ask him to repeat it. I sat there, feeling colder and colder, until I was so cold I had to move to stop from freezing.

"Would you like a drink before leaving?" I asked.

No tears, no scene.

He left, but kept coming back. Later, he had plenty of scenes at home. Alma loved the stage. She loved to make a spectacle of herself.

"So, what happened with the Japanese man?" No. 4 asked, a little impatient.

"The affair between Alma and the Japanese man lasted only a few days, because he had to leave for New York—the same vague 'business' excuse. What makes it memorable, besides that immodest avowal made by Alma, and which I'll keep for myself, is its consequence. Soon after his departure, Alma was the recipient of a very strange email with the subject line 'From the Wife of Mr. Takamatsu.' I remember the name to this day because it made me think, as it did Alma, of those emails sent 'From the Desk of Mr. ...,' an unfortunate Nigerian businessman, who was forced to go into exile and urgently needed my assistance and my bank account number to deposit all his money.

"I saw the email with my own eyes. It began, 'Dear Ms. Alma, you don't know me, but ...' I only recall the gist of the rest: I know you spent the last several days with my husband and I want to tell you to not trust him. Especially, don't trust him when he claims that he wants to open an English-language school and you should come to Japan to work for him. He's done that before with other women.'

"But the surprise came at the end of the message: the woman, who was traveling with her husband, wanted to meet Alma. I advised Alma categorically against meeting with her. There is nothing more distasteful than the fight of two women over a man. This is something you'd never see in France, except among immigrants. Once, on a street in Marseilles, I saw two African women who, after a very spirited vocal duel, used their purses to hit each other, and then proceeded to pull each other's hair, screaming like two wild cats. No, a French woman would invite the other woman over, and then they would decide together over dinner, like civilized people, how to share the man.

"But Alma, who's always been reckless and prey to a rather childish curiosity, ignored my advice and decided to meet the woman."

And so, I explained to No. 4 how afterward, all jittery and overexcited, Alma told me that, as happened with the man, the wife was at first unrecognizable. She'd seen her in Japan, when she was part of the shuffling-feet trio at Ninna-ji, and at the time, the woman left the impression of an ordinary, stale housewife with a pre–World War II gift for self-effacement. Now, the woman who got up to greet Alma in the Starbucks where they had agreed to meet looked, although not particularly attractive, as contemporary as any American woman her age, wearing a pair of blue jeans and sporting a cropped hairdo very different from her previous, silly, curler-puffed haircut. The woman behaved in a very civil manner, though she rarely looked Alma in the eye and seemed to wear a multilayered mask that gave off a waft of stuffy sadness like a coat kept for too long in a closet. The woman took charge of the conversation and, paradoxically, her imperfect English helped her because it allowed her to hide behind a maze of complex sentences she rarely finished and that contained a lot of incidentals and ellipses. The woman's stream of un-sentenced words made Alma think how true it was that grammar is the Law: it was as if by not finishing her sentences, the woman kept herself outside of any regulation and could not be touched by anything. At the end of half an hour it was still unclear what the woman wanted, except to "warn" Alma against the man's lack of scruples. In her own wifely way, the woman was discreet because she never questioned Alma about her doings

with her husband, to whom she referred as "Mr. Takamatsu."
Alma, less discreet, asked her why she referred to her husband
in this way; to which the woman answered, sincerely surprised,
"Why, it's his name!" There were only two instances in the
woman's wordiness that caught Alma's attention: when she used
the word "dangerous," and when she said, with a sudden veil
of melancholy descending over her face, that "the previous girl,
also an American, didn't end well." Alma didn't ask who the girl
was and why she didn't end well, but took note of it.

Exactly two days after Alma met the Japanese businessman's
wife, she received an email from him in which he warned her
about his wife's jealousy and pathological duplicity. He used the
same word to describe his wife that she had used to describe
him: "dangerous."

About a week later, Alma showed the first signs of her
breakdown. It may have been a coincidence, but even so, this
episode must have at least intensified the crisis. The Architect
told me that she refused to see anyone and was in her room
all the time, crying. Once, when they finally managed to have a
conversation, she told him between sobs that she felt she could
no longer grasp reality, and that, instead of being a continuum
of things and people interacting with each other, reality had
become for her a checkered cloth in which the black and white
squares were disconnected, forever enclosed in their loneliness.

"I don't know for sure how the story with the Japanese
man ended, because Alma never confided in me again. I tend to
believe it didn't end there, since half a year later she asked for a
divorce. And, as far as I know, she hadn't met you at the time,
although I might be wrong, of course."

"Alma and I met after she was separated, and we began to
date just barely before her divorce was officially pronounced.
You seem to imply that …"

"Oh, no, no, I am not implying anything. All I meant to say is that I am only an outsider, so I can only give a peripheral view of the situation. I have no reason not to believe you, in which case my suspicion that Alma's relationship with the Japanese man might have played a role in her divorce is probably justified. And in that case, chances are that her disappearance is connected to that man. After all—forgive me for pointing out the obvious—she's only known you for a few months."

"Are you saying that she left me *for him*?"

"Oh, I am not *saying* anything. I can only make suppositions based on the fragmentary knowledge I have. I am only suggesting this as a possibility—remember, *you wanted to know*, and I am telling you what I know. Of course, there is also the man's wife, let's not forget the wife, who complicates things even more, so in the end, she, I mean Alma, might come back to you. Well, I'm afraid I've told you all, and more, than I know, and our conversation is drawing to a close. All I know is that those fears of yours that something bad might have happened to Alma are—forgive me!—silly. I said it before, and I'll say it again: you people watch too many violent movies. You like to play with demons, like children. For better or worse, reality is always simpler: the woman, Alma, I mean, is having an affair. Be a little patient, and eventually, she'll reach out to you, one way or another. And, if I may give you a bit of advice: an affair is not the end of the world. If she is still willing to come back to you, don't be stubborn and proud! Don't say no! You'll regret it later."

When I finished, the man stood there, staring ahead somewhere into the distance, without giving any sign that he was ready to leave. He drew in a deep breath and looked me in the eye for a second, brow furrowed, pensive; then, he turned and began to walk toward the door, stopped again abruptly, and, facing me, said:

"You're lucky you've learned to master English so well."

"Lucky? How so?"

"Well, you have so many ideas and are so eager to express them. What would you have done if you only had French at your disposal? I mean, everybody knows what a poor language French is! Scholars who have compared the vocabulary used in a play by Shakespeare and one by Racine have concluded that the latter used a third as many words as the former. But no one has put it better than Keats: 'French is perhaps the poorest language ever spoken since the jabbering in the Tower of Babel!'"

With this, he gave me a large grin, and walked out the door.

Alma

Rumor has it that you've been talking to my exes, trying to "understand" me and "make sense" of my disappearance. (Yes, even where I am now, in this limbo, waiting to be sent to Paradise or Hell, there are rumors, which, moreover, are amplified by the fact that in limbo one is alone, and the rumors are bouncing against the walls of one's head.) And in the process you've been served, no doubt, some dubious stories. If you were so curious about your predecessors, the simplest thing would have been to ask me. I'll try to satisfy your curiosity, though I'm still not sure I'll ever send you this letter. More precisely, I'm not sure I'll ever finish it, and if I do, whether there will still be an *I* to mail it.

Let's go back to that faraway summer when, armed with a suitcase and a backpack under an endless turquoise sky that reflected an equally endless countryside, I moved up and down the map of France, searching for something without features but with enough gravity to keep me down to earth. At the time I still believed that certain places and stones can incarnate for us the lost Garden of Eden, and thus, fill the elusive dreams we all have with the flesh of (an alleged) reality. I can tell you about the nuns and the stones, and the monks and the stones, too, though, frankly, the monks were a lot less interesting. Or, better said, it's not that they were less interesting; rather, their personalities seemed to have been eroded by the continuous contact with the age-old stone walls, and all that was left of them were gray shadows drifting to and fro under protective hoods, while the women still preserved some variety, though it's possible that the men were more cautious in my presence, and therefore more phantomlike.

The nuns of Rouen were quite something! I took my meals with them in the dining room near the kitchen, so I was able to observe them at leisure. There was Sister A., a tall woman with glasses who held a PhD, and who, like a detective smelling a criminal as soon as he lays eyes on him, told me, "I know you are here for our *madeleines*." Then, there was Sister R., a very tiny old woman with goofy features, resembling one of the Seven Dwarves, who always appeared in the cracked door as soon as I entered the dining room in the afternoon to make myself a cup of tea, as if to say, "I'm watching you!" By the way, all French monasteries have the same bad Nescafé, Lipton, and chamomile tea, cubed sugar and powdered milk, which they keep in their old-fashioned wooden cupboards together with their earthenware and porcelain bowls and plates. Next to the cupboards, one can usually find a long walnut table with wooden benches, and on the table a carafe of water and a bottle of cider. By the door there is often a table with an electric kettle on it, or else a rolling cart on which the meals are brought from the kitchen.

This is the space I first explored each time I arrived at a new monastery, after leaving the luggage in my room. I would

arrive in the evening or late afternoon, and the *soeur hôtellière*
would show me the premises, and then leave me on my own in
the dining room. After all the hours spent on the train and in
train stations with the hectic maneuvering they imposed on one,
the dining room became for me a haven of order and quiet, a
gift I was awarded at the end of a long ordeal. The silence was so
thick it was almost tangible, and the slanted orange light of late
afternoon squeezing itself through the shades and landing on
the dark wood lent the gift a golden aura. The soft glow of these
sun-filtered afternoons reminded me of Tanizaki's notes on the
beauty of shadows and their importance in Japanese architecture.
Paradoxically, it was in these old Western monasteries that I
encountered the closest representation of Tanizaki's theory of
shadows, not in Japanese temples. It was truly ironic, considering
that he opposes the aesthetic of Western brightness and glorious
whiteness to the Japanese predilection for darkness and aged,
black lacquered surfaces, which appear to be melting into their
surroundings while capturing the interplay of the neighboring
shadows and turning them into shimmering rivers.

The *soeur hôtellière* of Jouarre was much more businesslike
than the one in Rouen, and for good reason. The abbey had more
than ten guests, some of them regulars who came there every
summer for "spiritual renewal." The glass cloister contrasted
with the one in Rouen, which had been plunged in semidarkness
and cold dampness, and, sparkling with joyous light, felt more
like a greenhouse than a cloister. As the Sister led the way out
into the garden, a multitude of red and white roses welcomed
us. After a week of constant rain in Rouen, so much sun and
color felt like the blinding brightness one experiences when
exiting a tunnel. Although the garden was inside a rectangle, the
garden itself was round, circled by a path of gravel that led to
one of the dorms.

It was dinnertime, so I left my luggage by the dining room door and followed the Sister inside. Seated at a long table covered with a white tablecloth were six men and women engaged in casual conversation, which was interrupted by the Sister, who introduced me, saying I'd "come all the way from America." Unable to get over the enormity of this word, "America," the Sister kept repeating it and, giggling, immediately covered her mouth in embarrassment. She then began to explain, with a schoolgirl's enthusiasm, "Today is our most important day of the year: the day of St. Benoît, our patron." Indeed, the table was set as for a holiday, with two bottles of wine, besides the customary cider, mashed potatoes, meatballs, peas, and carrot salad.

Everyone, save for a very old woman in a wheelchair, turned in my direction, and once I was seated, they began to ask me questions about "America." There was a slender, middle-aged woman with glasses who taught English at the Sorbonne and came there every summer; a couple in their early forties, exuding an aura of paper-thin asexuality, who spent their summers traveling to various monasteries; a woman in black in her early seventies with a severe expression, who kept silent the whole time; and a woman who must have been in her mid-forties, with very dark, short hair, olive skin, and the features of an indomitable Italian matriarch, but who was probably French, because she identified herself as Patrice. When the dessert we all owed to St. Benoît—crème caramel and strawberries—was brought on a tray by an unsmiling nun, the woman in black offered to make coffee, and no one said no. Then, with the cups of coffee before us, we continued our on-and-off chatter until the bells rang the *complies*, and everybody got up. In my usual, leisurely style, I stayed behind and, when everybody else but Patrice was out, after making sure that no one else could hear, she said:

"I don't really feel like going to the *complies*. Would you like to take a walk?"

I often wondered what my life would have been like had I said no. It's strange how much the major events in our life depend on trivial things like that.

We walked on the gravel path alongside the hawthorn hedges lining it, and paused for a minute to watch a nun standing in the distance, erect like a dry, leafless branch.

"*Madame se tient trop debout dans la prairie* ... Do you know this line?" asked Patrice in French, after having spoken a hesitant, guttural English.

"Of course. Rimbaud."

"Very good."

She spoke like a teacher, and, as it turned out, she *was* a high-school teacher of Italian.

"I knew you must be Italian. Your features ..."

"But I'm not. I am one hundred percent French. Well, as hundred per cent as we all are. We are all mixed, in the end."

Now that she was speaking French, she spoke too fast for me, so I had to make an effort to follow her words.

"I have a brother who is half American," Patrice continued.

"Really?"

"Yes, his father was American. We have the same mother."

"Does he live in France?"

"Yes. As a matter of fact, I am going to see him after I leave Jouarre. But tell me, what made you come here?"

Patrice had an abrupt way of changing the subject and of making inquiries, and almost any statement she made expressed an unambiguous opinion or judgment about something. This, I would come to realize in the next several days. That evening, she was in one of her rare lyrical moods, which expressed itself in a euphoric desire to contemplate, and talk about, nature. We began to play a game in which Patrice would say the name of a plant in French and then ask me to say it in English.

"*Aubépines.*"

"Hawthorns."

"*Buissons.*"

"Shrubs."

"*Eglantine.*"

"Wild rose."

"Are you Catholic?" Patrice suddenly asked.

Taken by surprise, I answered, "Yes," then "No," and finally, I stammered something unintelligible. As I stammered, Patrice looked me straight in the eye, with an inflexibility verging on cruelty. "Which is it, yes or no?" her eyes seemed to say.

"I wasn't baptized a Catholic," I finally said, and wanted to continue, but Patrice interrupted me with her usual brusqueness:

"You know, there isn't any shame in *not* being Catholic," and she gave a short laugh. "I, for one, no longer consider myself Catholic, though culturally speaking I am and will remain Catholic until the day I die, of course. When I was in the States I met people who tried to convince me that one is what one chooses to be. I told them that I may choose to be a Buddhist, but my Catholic upbringing will still color all my new opinions whether I realize it or not. Americans are under the illusion that one can decide to embrace whatever culture one wants, as if 'culture' were a gown one puts on for a special occasion, and not the body under the gown that gives it shape. When I was in California, my yoga teacher, who saw herself as some kind of a Buddhist, kept blabbing about how one had to 'grow.' It didn't seem to cross her mind that 'growth' is a Christian value, and even more, a Protestant obsession, and that her 'Buddhism' was conceived in a Christian bed."

I wanted to voice my approval, but before I even opened my mouth, Patrice interrupted me:

"Oh, but I am talking like my compatriots! Americans this, Americans that…. You know, French people are very full of themselves, and think they are better than the 'Americans,' but *who* are the 'Americans'? My brother is an American, I think I told you."

"Didn't you say he lives in France?"

"Yes, he is a monk in a monastery near Poitiers. I'll see him next week."

I wanted to ask her what order her brother belonged to, and in what monastery, but once again, Patrice was faster.

"Oh, look at that marvelous sunset! *Oh, quelle splendeur! Quelle beauté! Quelle merveille!*"

Patrice had a low, masculine voice, so even when she produced exclamations and interjections—which, in the case of most people, are uttered at a higher pitch—her tone descended, as if she were making a categorical and indisputable judgment, rather than getting excited about a view. Her tone seemed divorced from her utterance—she said, *"Quelle splendeur!"* the way other people say, "What the hell!"—as if the form she briefly inhabited by getting excited couldn't adapt itself to the negative content she embodied by nature and temperament.

From then on, we took long daily walks between meals on the gravel path in the garden, or occasionally ventured outside the monastic domain, on the village's sleepy, uneventful streets. We spoke mostly in French, except when Patrice remembered she knew English, and then her abrupt switch translated into a strange combination of grammatically correct English utterances wrapped in a cloth of French vowels and inflexions. (Her English has improved considerably, by the way, since she's been living in the States.) Patrice had strong opinions about the Americans who spoke French with such unbearable accents—I was *not* one of them, she hastened to add—but she never gave me a chance to voice my own opinion about the French who spoke English. As the flow of words coming from Patrice never seemed to allow for an *exchange*, it occurred to me that the French have no respect for the ethics of *trade,* and that it was because of their lack of respect for this practice that, even in conversation, they could not obey the rule of a proper exchange. While for an American, a conversation is an act of linear, straight dealing—I give you something, you give me something back—for a Frenchman, a conversation is an act of subterfuge, of stratagems made of devious *artifice* through which one fights for power, and not for a *fair* acquisition. In other words, what for one is ethics, for the other is aesthetics—though Patrice would have probably used the word "bigotry" for the former, and she would have added, "Beware of the American who lectures you on the greatness of the capitalist market, for under that umbrella, in ninety per cent of cases, hides a religious bigot."

It was tiring and, frankly, exasperating, to play the role of the listener with Patrice, vainly attempting to insert a word, to start a sentence that would never be finished, so after a while I gave up and let Patrice be in charge of her monodialogues. We were sitting on a bench in the enclosed garden when I made this decision, but ironically, I realized almost immediately that Patrice had been unusually silent that afternoon. It was as if the world's engine had stopped running: an eerie quiet enveloped everything, interrupted every now and then by a rumor in the trees, like the hushed sound of shuffled leaves.

"You are very quiet today," noted Patrice.

Is she kidding?! I almost snapped. Instead I began, "I think I've been very quiet," but before I could add, "ever since I met you," Patrice interrupted me:

"I have an idea. What are you planning to do after Jouarre?"

I told her that I was planning to visit the *Monastère de la Visitation* in Caen, and the *Monastère des Carmélites* in Avranches, and after that, I wasn't sure, maybe go to the Riviera.

"Why don't you come to Ligugé? The Saint-Martin Abbey is one of the most beautiful abbeys in France, and my brother will see that you are given a room with your own bathroom. True, their food is much worse than here, if they still have the same cook. The last time I was there I lost four pounds in two weeks. Boiled green beans, vegetable stock, and boiled potatoes—that's their idea of a meal. But there are some perks.... My brother can tell you everything you want to know about the abbey's history. He has a degree in history, you know."

"How old was he when he decided to become a monk?"

"Oh, young. Very young," Patrice answered vaguely. Then, turning brusquely to face me, she uttered with conviction, "My brother is a saint."

I would have liked to ask what qualified her brother to be deemed worthy of such a title, but I didn't have time, because Patrice stood up:

"Not like me," she went on. "I left home when I was eighteen, and it was not to behave like a saint. My father was very strict. You don't know how lucky you are, because you weren't raised Catholic."

"But how about your brother? Isn't *he* lucky?"

"I told you. My brother is a saint."

"You said you have different fathers, but you lived with your father."

"Yes, my mother left when I was nine. One night she came home, poured herself a glass of Bordeaux, lit a cigarette, and told my father, 'Jacques, I am leaving you'. My father pushed aside the newspaper he'd been reading ever since I was born—

but barely, as if to make sure he could go back to his reading after my mother finished her speech—and looked at her with an interrogative expression. My mother gave him a big smile: 'He is your opposite in every way.'

"'You mean he is poor, handsome, young and stupid?' My father said. 'Well, congratulations.' And he went on reading the paper.

"My mother left the next day. Her future husband was, indeed, poor, handsome, and younger than my father, but far from stupid. At the time, he lived on an Indian reservation in Oregon, working on a book about American Indians, though he himself was Caucasian. A harsh place to live—I visited them a year later. I never thought one could live in such poverty in the States. I felt sorry for my mother, but I decided to live with my father. Then, as now, I valued a clean toilet more than anything else. Believe me, nothing is worth more than a clean toilet, especially not a man! They didn't even have electricity or running water in that place. That's where my brother was born."

"How long did they live there?" I asked, but at that moment the bells tolled. Making a grimace, Patrice said that she felt obligated to attend vespers prayer because she had skipped mass that day, and didn't want the sisters to doubt her devotion. She said the words "doubt my devotion" with her customary mocking laugh, and took off immediately.

The next day I wanted to resume our conversation, but Patrice had invited another woman along, a newly arrived guest. The woman, who was about Patrice's age, maybe older, and, judging from her bland clothes and soporific features, very likely a pious Catholic, made me think of someone fed on ragout and porridge, playing Chopin every night in a gray hemp gown. The conversation turned into mindless chatter, though the new guest wasn't much of a talker. It was Patrice who, for some reason, felt obligated to play the hostess, and gave the woman the same thorough report on the sisters she had given me. It was hard not to notice that she was treating the new guest with the same exclusive attention she had previously lavished on me, so I felt betrayed, especially since this woman was as gray and self-effaced as a stone on the gravel path we walked on every day. That's why, when Patrice reiterated her invitation that I come to the Abbey of Saint Martin in Ligugé, I answered coldly that I couldn't promise anything. I had reserved a room at the Monastère de la Visitation in Caen, and after that I intended to go to Avranches.

"Well, if you change your mind, I'll be there for the next three weeks," Patrice said.

At the *Monastère de la Visitation* I was welcomed by Sister Jeanne, who must have been about seventy years old, though she had no wrinkles, and her energy could put to shame a twenty-year-old. She was short, with a round face; big, candid eyes; and a very active mouth. Sister Jeanne was in the paradoxical situation of having embraced a vocation that demanded her retreat from the world, yet, at the same time, of harboring a very sociable temperament and an immense desire to communicate. Our sister liked empty chatter and, had she embraced a more mundane career, she would have made a great gossip columnist. At least, this is what I thought when, however hard I tried to get away under the pretext of tiredness, I realized that nothing could deter Sister Jeanne once she began talking about a certain Sister Léonie:

"You *have* to see Sister Léonie. We are so proud to have her here."

I was about to say that I would be happy to meet Sister Léonie later, before or after dinner, but Sister Jeanne had made up her mind and, grabbing me by the hand, led me down the spiral stairs, through the kitchen, then a corridor through which our steps reverberated with a cold echo, and then down some uneven steps, until we finally stopped before an arched wooden door. Sister Jeanne took out a ring of heavy keys, and the door opened onto a well-lit, almost bare room with a catafalque against one of the walls and a glass display case positioned perpendicular to it.

"This is Sister Léonie's room," Sister Jeanne said in a tremulous voice.

I peeked at the glass display, and identified a comb ("Sister Léonie's comb"), an old Bible ("Sister Léonie's Bible"), and a photo of a young woman ("Sister Léonie at twenty-two").

"These are Sister Léonie's things," Sister Jeanne added, visibly moved. I didn't know what the appropriate thing to say was, so I just cleared my throat, and watched Sister Jeanne move closer to the catafalque on which lay a woman's sculpted likeness. As Sister Jeanne murmured, "And this is our dear Léonie," I too moved closer, intending to ask a question, but noticed that my hostess was still, with her eyes closed. I waited a minute for the moment of silence to pass, but the moment turned into minutes, until, eventually, I began to wonder whether Sister Jeanne had fallen asleep. I cleared my throat again, this time louder, and Sister Jeanne started, looking around with a confused expression.

"When did she die?" I asked.

"Who?"

"Sister Léonie!"

"Oh! 1941."

* * *

The next day after breakfast I heard a light knock at the door, and when I opened, Sister Jeanne's gray silhouette appeared in the crack, with her round, childish face hiding behind a large smile.

"I brought you this to read while you are here," she said, handing me a book. Catching a glimpse of the title, *La Vie de Sainte Léonie*, I sighed and took the book.

"I wrote it," Sister Jeanne continued, with a shy giggle.

"Oh."

"There are only three copies, so you shouldn't lose it."

After Sister Jeanne left the room, a sudden thunder split the skies, and the daylight turned gray. A chilly draft blew open the windows with a loud bang and the air rushed in, dense and heavy, and for about ten minutes the sky was suspended in indecision, then it made up its mind with a roar. The rain began to pour down and the air grew colder, autumnlike. I hastened to close the windows, took off my shoes, and returned to bed under the cheap, monastic blankets. There are very few things I enjoy more than the patter of rain on a window, so I lay in bed listening to it and, almost unconsciously, I found myself reading the beginning of *The Life of Sainte Léonie*, but before even finishing the first sentence, I was sound asleep.

The rain went on and on, with occasional short breaks. At times it seemed as if the skies could no longer contain all the water they had accumulated, and the rain kept falling, not by the drop but by the bucket. An autumnal chill settled in, although it was mid-summer, and the objects seemed to shrink the way certain animals and body parts do in cold water. After spending four days intermittently daydreaming by the foggy window and dreaming under the covers, I called the monastery in Avranches and asked if I could come earlier than agreed upon. A hesitant voice asked me to hold on, and then, after a minute or two, came back: "Sure, you'll be our only guest."

Sister Jeanne didn't hide her disappointment when I announced I would leave early. She looked like a child prematurely aged on whom a mean adult had played a bad trick. "But, Alma, why?" she kept asking. "Wasn't the food good? Wasn't the room comfortable?" I tried to reassure her that everything had been to my liking, but the sister didn't seem convinced. When, before getting into the taxi, I handed her the book back, Sister Jeanne adopted the pose of a heroine ready to sacrifice for the good of the community: "No, *you* take it with you! I insist! This way you'll remember us."

Contemplating the large, four hundred-page paperback in my lap on the way to the train station, I tried to come up with a reasonable solution for its disappearance. On the one hand, I had no intention of carrying that ridiculous object with me for the rest of my trip; on the other, I valued books too much to simply throw it away. The only possible way out was to give it to someone, but to whom? Well, of course! I could give it to the *Soeur Hôtellière* in Avranches! This meant I had to carry it and hold on to it on the train, when I would have loved to just drop it right then and there and let the taxi driver deal with it. But once I arrived in Avranches, I succumbed to an immense lassitude that stopped me from handing it to the Sister. I was in no mood to come up with an explanatory lie and felt an infinite boredom at the thought that within the next several days I'd have to go through the same ritual all over again. Even the Sister—apparently, the same one I'd spoken with on the phone—reminded me of Soeur Jeanne's mannerisms, though physically she was the exact opposite: tall, with a horselike face. As the *Soeur Hôtellière* welcomed me, another, much older sister—dark, dry, with the wary gaze of a Sicilian mother-in-law—stood silently aside and kept her old-woman's silence even when the *Soeur* turned to her to say, "Alma has come all the way from America." The *Soeur* repeated, "America," widening her eyes and shaking her head from side to side to make sure the older woman understood that this was no small thing, and eventually, the old woman responded by slightly projecting her jaw forward and giving a barely visible nod with her head. Then the two of them stood there, wrapped in the echo of that ungraspable word that still floated in the air: "America."

And then, there I was again, following the long-faced sister, who was showing me the premises, and up a flight of wooden stairs—which, unlike the stairs in the other places, were straight—and through the hall to my room, which was as unpretentious as my previous rooms, but sunnier and cozier. I threw myself on the bed, thankful that the ordeal of carrying my suitcase was over, and ready to enjoy a long rest, but as soon as I put my head on the pillow, there was a knock at the door. It was the Sister, apologizing both in words and with her long face.

"We'd be very happy if you could join us at the *complies*," she said.

There was something humble about her demeanor, in spite of her height, as if she were constantly apologizing to someone. I was prepared to refuse, but I wasn't ready to say it to that meek face, so, with a sigh, I told the Sister I would be there. I spent the next two days trying to escape that circle of submissive-looking sisters, who were constantly inviting me to pray with them, but since I was too weak to leave the monastery, and even putting my clothes on left me so exhausted I was on the brink of collapsing, I had no option but to join them.

The third day started with a horrible headache, and when I didn't show up for breakfast, the horse-faced Sister knocked at the door. She grew very agitated when, with a hoarse voice and feverish breath, I whispered from under the blanket, "I'm sick." As the Sister paced up and down, producing interjections and exclamations to manifest her worried state, I understood that I was in a position of power and it would have been stupid not to take advantage of it. I told the Sister that I absolutely had to call my husband in the States, and she helped me get up and walk a few steps down the hall until we reached a table with an antediluvian phone on it.

It was my husband who convinced me to stay in France and go meet Patrice at the Saint-Martin Abbey in Ligugé. When I arrived, I was greeted by her and a monk whose face was hidden under his cloak's gray hood. As he extended his hand to shake mine, he raised his head and the hood slid back. I still don't know what to call the feeling I had then. It was an instant knowledge that he would play an essential role in my life, a strong sense of familiarity, as if I'd known him, but couldn't remember in what capacity. This feeling was all the more strange since he, although extremely polite, looked at me without giving any indication that he was seeing me. I had never seen a gaze of such blue, nonhuman intensity, which, instead of penetrating what it touched, glided over things and people alike—the gaze of a blind man or a seer. After being in his presence for a few minutes, I began to experience an unexpected surge of anger: I felt like pulling up his eyelids to force him to *look at me,* or like yelling at him, "Who do you think you are to ... to ..." To what? To have this kind of detached gaze? It was inhuman for someone to be like that. This must have been the sainthood Patrice was talking about, but in that case, being a saint was equivalent to being a bloodless corpse. Other monks and nuns I had met in the States or in France often had that pose of detachment, but one could tell it was only an artifice as necessary in the construction of their monastic persona as sexiness is for a Hollywood actress. With him, on the other hand, there was no artifice, no pretense, no surface. Everyone is made of an inside and an outside, and it's usually by looking one in the eye that you can catch a glimpse of their inner world. But with him it was just the opposite: when you looked into those opaque blue eyes, you bumped into a wall of impenetrable strangeness. Even in his sister's presence, he appeared the same. If it hadn't been for the words they exchanged, and which revealed a common past and interests, you'd never have imagined that they were more than strangers. They talked about music and books I wasn't familiar with—classical and religious music, theologians and philosophers—and in those moments I felt as out of place as in my first year of college when I used to hang out with grad students who kept repeating the same French names over and over—Bataille was one of them, and I knew enough French to know it meant "battle," but what battle were they talking about? Patrice and her brother never attempted to include me in the conversation—he, because he didn't even notice I was there; she, because ... well, because she's French.

After Patrice left, the Monk and I continued to meet in the library, a communal room with dark, upholstered chairs, a long, brown, fake-leather couch, and shelves lining the walls with books that triggered in me no desire to read, and which were the kind of books Patrice and her brother read. This is where the monks of yore had studied arithmetic, geometry, music, and astronomy; that is, all the sciences pertaining to numbers, rhythm, and proportion.

"The world breathed a different order then," the Monk once said, "a world of which only these walls are left, the only sign that once there was a God. For this is what a monastery ultimately does: it takes the space from the outside—the space where an alien God is hidden—and brings it within. This is the reason why even atheists find monasteries so peaceful: there is no divorce between what's inner and what's outer."

Occasionally, another guest would come in looking for a book, or simply to read the paper and sip his or her afternoon tea by the big walnut table, but never a monk, unless by chance or in passing. At the time, I didn't realize how deeply satisfying those afternoons were; it's only the passage of time that, with its slanted aura of light and soothing tick-tock, has given them a sepia quality, so when I think of them now, I can't imagine greater happiness than that of the woman I was then. Sometimes, when the guest would stick around for too long, the Monk and I would get up and go out for a walk, so in my mind the old books, the dark chairs, and the summer garden are all linked together, like indispensable ingredients in a recipe for happiness.

One day we were sitting on the bench outside, and I finally got the nerve to do something I was dying to do: I kissed him. Well, not really kissed—simply touched his lips and waited for him to kiss me back. But he just sat there—it was the strangest thing. He neither kissed me nor pulled back. He stayed like that, barely breathing. I thought that maybe he was teasing me, but after a minute or so it was clear that he didn't know what to do. I almost burst out laughing, but managed to control myself, turned my head away, and stood up. Now, when I think of this scene, when I see him on that bench with his lips tightly closed on my lips, like a toddler learning the mystery of two lips pressing on a cheek or on two other lips, I think that this may be the dearest memory I have.

And now, you may keep it for me because in this room, surrounded by white, bare walls, all I want is to purge myself of all the memories until all that's left of me is a thin, transparent membrane, which will slowly fade away into pure nothingness. Have you ever thought that a hotel room is the closest thing to a monastery? They are both impersonal spaces, the latter insofar as it welcomes the impersonality of the divine, and the former because it's made for *no one* in particular. I came here in order to be no one, and what better place to be no one than a hotel in Tokyo?

I confess, though, I'm not entirely sure I'm ready to disappear. I thought I was, but then, thinking of what the Architect and Patrice must have told you, I would have loved to be a fly on the wall. Let's play a guessing game, shall we? I bet Patrice told you about the coffee cup episode. This is a perfect example of how "the facts" don't mean anything. Factually, what she told you is true. But what was missing from her story is that element of ambiguity that infuses reality and which Patrice is absolutely incapable of seeing. It is true that for a while I suspected the Architect of nurturing ... hmm ... poisonous thoughts, so to speak, about me, and there were moments when I believed that these thoughts were ready to materialize, so I was constantly on guard. But when I asked Patrice to drink from my cup—the cup he'd filled—*in that moment* I was both within the moment, suspecting him and subjecting them both to a test, *and* outside of it. When I ordered her to drink, I suddenly stepped out of the scene, I could see myself as caught in a TV drama and, as such, infinitely ridiculous, so, as I uttered those words, they were being spoken by a character I was playing and who was as remote from me as any character on a screen or a stage. In a word, what I did then was "theater."

The Architect told you, I'm sure, that I was seriously mixed-up, and that in my fantasy world I was imagining that he wanted to wall me up like a certain mason from a Balkan myth, am I right? Pretty crazy, indeed. But what he forgot to tell you is that, when he built our Tower, he buried my husband's shadow in it. Burying a human shadow in the foundation of a building was a custom that at some point in history had replaced human sacrifice—a more humane version of the same idea. I didn't know anything at the time, of course, I discovered this later, more exactly, the night before I left him—the Architect, I mean.

He was working late, and I entered his office to fetch something, and spotted an old notebook lying on the floor under his desk chair. Most of the pages in it had technical drawings and measurements, interrupted here and there by a short laundry list—typical of him. I was about to put it on his desk when my gaze fell on the Monk's name, and next to it, his measurements: weight and height. I was intrigued, of course, and turned the page: there lay a drawing of our Tower with the sketch of a man outside of it, and his shadow lengthening all the way to the entrance. And another drawing with the same Tower, man and shadow, this time from a different angle, near a different part of the Tower. The man was very sketchy, but under the drawing one could read the following quote:

> The buried shadow is a symbolic sacrifice meant to solidify the foundations of a new edifice by incorporating a human life in it. It was sometimes believed that the person whose shadow was buried will give up the ghost soon thereafter. It is easy to see how the shadow and the ghost (i.e., the spirit) are one and the same, so much so that one could say that giving up one's shadow is giving up one's spiritual double, that is, one's self.

I know you don't believe in this kind of childish sorcery, and neither do I. And the Architect is the last person one would expect to be dealing in such nonsense (to use a word he often employs). But I also know that he has an overinflated sense of self, and would do anything—and I mean *anything*—to raise his profile as an architect. And if that takes being initiated in some medieval craftsmen's guild, or even going to a fortune teller and sacrificing a rooster or a shadow, so be it.

I stood there with the notebook in hand, trembling. Whether one believes in such things or not is not the issue here. What counts is that this man *buried* the man I loved. I felt an overpowering wave of nausea and, as soon as I was able to pull myself together, I began packing.

Now, my "fantasy world," as the Architect calls my intuitions about him, doesn't seem quite as far-fetched, does it? I still believe that, if he could, he would wall me up—*me*, not my shadow—and if he hasn't done it so far it is simply out of fear of the law. And his accomplice-in-spirit, Patrice, is part of that race of women who seem made of iron, fiercely independent, until one day they meet a man who succeeds in bending their will, and then they turn into the most pathetic, laughable creatures. This is what happened to Patrice after she met the Architect. I won't hide from you that I'm curious to know what she had to say to you. That's because she never just "says" things; she states them with the implacable confidence of a seer. But a seer is an impartial viewer, while Patrice can't help being very partial when it comes to me. You must have noticed that her partiality comes from the special bond she has with the Architect and the Monk. She has a double reason to hate me—and, as far as everyone can tell, she does—but I'll tell you a secret: what she hates more than anything is that, in fact, she can't hate me, and I'm sure Patrice herself, who values reason above all, must be puzzled by this. If she hated me, I'd be the first to know. One knows these things. I'm sure she tried to convince you that I left the Architect because I was crazy—"had a nervous breakdown," as she delicately calls it—but failed to mention her own efforts directed at the destruction of my marriage. I made the mistake once of telling her that I was *rendez-vous*-ing with a fellow I'd met in Japan at Ninna-ji, who was visiting Boston on business, and from there she concocted a whole adulterous scenario. I know it because the Architect alluded to it, and she was the only person in the world to whom I had talked about that.

Since we are on the topic of the man from Ninna-ji, I should tell you that the strangest thing happened—something so uncanny I'm not even sure what meaning to assign to it, if any. It so happened that we were again at Ninna Temple at the same time—he always comes there once a year with his wife and his mother, but this time the two women had left earlier—and we decided to travel together back to Tokyo. We took the train, and when we arrived in Tokyo we discovered that he lived in the same neighborhood my hotel is in, so we took a cab together. Before the cab dropped me off, we exchanged phone numbers and agreed to call each other.

The next day I was taking one of those afternoon naps that are so sweet in an impersonal hotel room in the middle of an unknown, bustling city, doubly suspended in a void, within the dream, and within the city—two dreamscapes revolving around the room's axis—when all of a sudden something happened within my dream: a dark shadow lengthened inside the room until it covered the floor, and then crept onto my bed, moving from my feet upward. When it reached my chest it grew so heavy I could hardly breathe, and when, in the end, it stretched to my throat and I felt my chest would explode, I woke up bathed in sweat. The room had gotten a little darker but otherwise it was just as peaceful and welcoming as when I'd gone to bed.

The sensation of a barely avoided danger was still throbbing in my throat when the phone rang. Or, maybe it was the other way around: maybe the phone rang first and woke me up, and in the two or three seconds that its ring lasted, the dream's lingering images stayed on my retina. I answered, still dazed. It was the Japanese man. Barely able to open my mouth, I jotted down the address of a restaurant not far from my hotel. I hung up and sat staring ahead for a few seconds, waiting for the aftertaste of my slumber to fade away. Instead, the sensation of danger grew even stronger, and this time it seemed as if it came directly from the phone. I could tell that a panic attack or a new bout of depression was just around the corner, and the only way to fight them was by forcing myself to get out of bed and out of the room. When I get in one of those states my body turns into an electric receptor that catches any sign of danger within a ten-mile radius, and at that moment every cell in my body was telling me to not leave the room. I was paralyzed with fear, yet I knew that the only way to fight it was to get out. And so I did.

I found the building fairly quickly, but when I opened the door and saw the sign in both Japanese and English, "To restaurant," with an arrow pointing in the direction of the narrow flight of stairs descending into the basement, I paused, warily. The stairs were dark and dingy, but at their end one could see a beam of light and hear voices and the clatter of glasses and plates. Again my body sensed danger, and I just stood there arguing with myself. I decided that the only way to vanquish the dark shadow inside me was by stepping outside of myself, so I went down the stairs. And then the beam of light turned into dozens of small candles illuminating a huge dining hall with round tables and a few private booths along the wall, and the voices were now a curtain of sounds from which banging pots and clattering glasses hung like tassels. Some kind of decorative waterfall ran on the black granite wall to my right, with ribbons of clear water streaming down and filling a little pond in which goldfish and pebbles were clearly visible.

As I entered, my first thought was, *This place is too elegant for my pocket.* My second thought, after seeing two hostesses with bright red, tight miniskirts, and crimson, siliconed lips: *no, elegant is not the word.* I told one of the hostesses that I was supposed to meet Mr. Takamatsu and, after checking a list, she asked me to follow her. Only then did I notice that all the women, hostesses and customers alike, wore tiny miniskirts or dresses, high heels and low décolletages. I was the only one in jeans—black, but still—and I was feeling slightly odd. The hostess led me to a private booth and my date showed up as soon as she left.

Each time I try to rewind the film of the night's events, when I get to the part where we start drinking, the film plays in slow motion, ever more garbled and blurrier until it fades into misty whiteness. I see a male hand pour drinks from a bottle, but no faces, though the presence of countless faces is palpable in the smoke-thick air. The male hand takes mine, and I have the strange sensation that our hands are melting into each other. I try to tell him this, but as I open my mouth, my tongue feels incredibly heavy, and then I think, *what's the point.* I keep trying to feel my hand, but all I can summon is an overwhelming lethargy pulsing through my veins, and a soft absence instead of hands. The hostess arrives like a red apparition and places a platter on the table. I look at the platter, fascinated by the dishes' vivid colors, and see how the colors slide away in splashes of red, orange, bright blue, and liquid green. I am about to say to the man next to me—whose name I can't remember—"Look, what beautiful colors," but in that instant he says, laughing, "I'm going to eat you up," and he bites my hands, jokingly. I laugh, too, but then my hand disappears into his mouth. First the hand, then the wrist. I panic, so I pull my hand out, and there it is, whole again. He laughs, and wants to bite my hand again, but something feels wrong. I feel as if I am about to remember something, that out of the kaleidoscope of colors and voices around me a shape is about to emerge. I make an effort to let the shape pull itself together amid all the jumble, and little by little I see a man's arm with very dark hairs. The arm belongs to the man next to me, the Japanese man whose name I can't remember. What does this man remind me of? Dark. A dark man.

Beware of a dark man. I see my hand in a woman's large, calloused hand; a pack of cards lying on the table; a checkered tablecloth with crumbs on it; the woman saying, "Beware of a dark man with a friendly face. He speaks a foreign language, rough as stone. He will try to do you harm. I see Death coming from him."

This memory occurred in what seemed like a moment of lucidity, though this would be an inaccurate description. It was as if my brain had acquired the penetrating vision of an owl that could bring clarity to the thickest night while my body lagged behind in a different universe, like a heavy log numbed by slumber and heat. I, who am, as they say, blind as a bat, could suddenly see the tiniest marks on people's faces, the skin's uneven, porous surface, crisscrossed by wrinkles like so many valleys of tears, and peppered with age spots. I could see the hidden wishes behind the liquid shimmering of the opaque eyes set in people's faces like two cases of jewelry, of which I was suddenly a master appraiser. I could see all this, yet I had no idea how and when this couple—a woman wearing the same crimson miniskirt as all the other women, and the man, older, in a black business suit—had come to our table. My vision was superhumanly clear, yet my understanding of things was incredibly muddled. The man and the woman seemed to have sprung out of the floor, but judging from the familiarity with which they addressed me, we must have talked for quite some time. I noticed that Mr. Takamatsu's left hand was resting on the woman's bared thigh. I have a very clear memory of how everybody's hands were positioned at that moment, yet I'm still not sure those two people really existed. At the time, they appeared real, of course. The man's face was pockmarked, and he exuded that repulsive ugliness I associate with a certain type of Japanese businessman. I think it was as I looked at him that I realized how much I disliked Mr. Takamatsu himself, and I experienced a visceral desire to get out of there. But Mr. Takamatsu was still holding my hand in his (right) hand; his left hand was still on the other woman's thigh. I knew he wouldn't let me go, so I had to lie. I said I had to go to the toilet, and as I got up, I sensed his gaze piercing my back. Instinctively, I grabbed my purse and walked barefoot, following the sign to the restroom. I don't know if you can imagine an adult learning to walk, but this is how I felt. It was a long, long walk, at times on a plush red rug, into which my feet sank, as in a meadow, and at times on the cool wooden floor, which my soles embraced with unusual thirst. I had no idea one could feel so intensely with one's feet. By the time I arrived in the dark, smelly hall where the restrooms and the payphones were located I had the impression I'd crossed into a whole other universe. Before me was the staircase leading to the outside world: I put my right foot on the first stair, and began climbing toward the glitter of intermittent pink and blue neon light.

I remember walking barefoot on the sidewalk and occasionally stepping on sharp objects, but I felt no pain. All I felt was the breeze in my hair, and the night pushing me from behind toward safety. I have no recollection of entering the hotel or my room. I woke up the next day sometime in the afternoon, in my evening clothes, and when I attempted to get up, the weight of my head pulled me back. My mouth was dry, and for an instant I couldn't find my tongue inside it. Something was wrong with my body, I thought. Alarmed, I began to move my limbs, one by one. Two legs, two arms, two hands. Everything seemed in place. Nothing hurt—apart from my head. When I finally managed to prop up my back against the pillow, I spotted my purse on the floor, and that brought back the first string of images. Little by little I recalled where I was and how I got there. I heaved a sigh of relief. Thank God, I was (still) *someone* (rather than no one). I still had a memory. And, then, I remembered *you*.

Or, rather, I remembered that there was someone out there who was you, but my memory of him was like that of people we'd known ages ago, and when an accident brings back their existence, we marvel at the strangeness of our ties, bewildered that there was a time when these people meant something to us. The more I thought about you, the more I thought not only about the stranger you had become but also about the person I myself had been. Such a strange thing, it seemed, to live outside this hotel room, move this way and that, worry about this or that other thing, which in the great scheme of things, meant nothing. "The great scheme of things!" *What was the great scheme of things? Could this hotel be part of the great scheme of things?* I began to laugh. Maybe I was losing my mind. I had to focus. I took the pen and a sheet of paper from the room's notepad and decided to write you a letter. Almost a week has passed since then. In the great scheme of things, a week is, of course, nothing. In the great scheme of things, the life of each of us is nothing. We all know this, yet we cling to dear life with an imbecilic determination. Maybe it's time for me to start paying attention to the great scheme of things. (As I'm writing this, a little bird sitting on my balcony rail has begun to chirp zestfully, deploying so much energy one would think it strongly disagrees.) Every day I spend hours staring at the wall before me—"meditating."

Is this paying attention to the great, or the small, scheme of things? I wonder. There is nothing closer to the great scheme of things than nothingness. I just realized this—just now, as I am writing these words. Don't we spend our entire lives moving slowly toward nothingness (all the while trying to postpone reaching it) as toward our own origin, and shouldn't we honor the mystery where we came from by spending as much time as possible in the proximity of nothingness? I could spend the rest of my life staring at this wall, and that would be a noble life. I would gradually leave behind me all the subjective, pitiful characteristics that make a "person," the gory flesh and blood that make a "life," and I would *whiten* myself like a tree once green that sublimates itself into white paper. Yes, I would become the wall that is now inside my eyes. What greater homage to the world around me than to become *it*? What greater victory against that silly husband of mine who thought *he* could wall *me* up than my willful immuring—not an immuring inside someone else's creation, but inside the blankest, most soulless place of all, a hotel room?

Last night I was lying in bed unsuccessfully trying to fall asleep, even after having applied the method the Architect taught me, of not only counting sheep but of visualizing them jumping one by one over an obstacle. Usually this works, but this time, after arriving in mid-air, each sheep remained suspended there, and the concentration it took to move the creature to the other side ended by dissipating my sleepiness. I was counting the ninety-something sheep when the phone rang. It was past midnight—and no one ever calls me here. I had been tempted to move to another hotel to avoid any possibility of contact from Mr. Takamatsu, but my shoes, left the next day after our dinner at the reception, remained his last attempt. Besides, the management has clear instructions to not forward me any calls. I was determined to let the phone ring, since it was very likely an error, but the sound was so piercing in the surrounding quiet, and the person at the other end so persistent, that I had no choice. I answered.

"Hello?"

The voice was that of a young woman, hesitant.

"Wrong number," I said, and was about to hang up, but she was faster.

"Please don't hang up!"

I recognized a Japanese accent.

"Who's this?"

"My name is Kotomi. I am your neighbor, next door at 651."

"I see. So, you're calling your neighbors to get to know them," I said, sarcastically.

"No . . . " she answered, ignoring my tone. "It's just that I stayed in your room two weeks ago. I asked them to give me another room because the shower wasn't working properly."

She was right. The shower produced an anemic trickle of water that would have deeply annoyed anyone else but me. I hate showers, and I take them only when forced to interact with other people.

"Have we met?" I asked.

"I've seen you. Twice. You had ordered room service and the door was open."

"OK, Kotomi. I'm very tired, so could you please get to the point: what do you want?"

It was her feminine voice and her softness—that Japanese female softness—that made me want to be rude to her. And I suppose I succeeded, because her tone became very apologetic.

"Oh, please excuse me. I didn't mean to disturb you. I was only calling because, you see, you don't know, but I think we have many things in common."

"Really?"

"Well, I get room service every day, too. And judging from the different times of day when I hear your TV, you, like me, must spend all your time in your room."

She had a point. But for some reason—her softness!—I didn't want to let her have it. What did she want? To be my friend because we both watched TV and had room service?

"Listen, Kotomi, you still haven't told me why you called."

"I'm sorry, I thought you understood. As I said, we are neighbors, and for our own personal reasons have locked ourselves up in these rooms, so I thought ..."

"You thought I needed a 'friend'! Well, I'm sorry to disappoint you, but I already have more friends than I need."

And I hung up. I hadn't spoken with anyone in days, so this human contact, combined with my outburst, gave me an adrenaline rush, or to put it more crassly, caused me a rush of pleasure. It was strange: I didn't normally take pleasure in being unkind, but this woman was asking for it. She reminded me of a fragile bird caught by the boys in our neighborhood in my early childhood. The boys amused themselves by catching little stray animals and birds, and torturing them. I fell asleep feeling the palpitating, wounded wing in my closed fist.

I spent the next day between *The Makioka Sisters*—which, alas, I still hadn't finished, despite having decided to try it again after putting it aside during my first trip to Ninna-ji— and TV soap operas interrupted by splashes of multicolored commercials, and hour-long episodes of drifting selflessness before the bare walls of cottoned silence. Only at the end of the day, as I lay in bed ready to start counting sheep again, did I remember Kotomi. At first, with bemused curiosity; but then, as I was counting my sheep, I realized that their soft features were those of a young Japanese woman: white-skinned, with the wide-open, naïve eyes of a sheep-like victim. I fidgeted, struggling to replace the sheep-woman with a more male-looking animal, but Kotomi-the-sheep refused to leave.

Exasperated, I turned on the light, picked up the phone, and dialed my neighbor's extension. She answered right away, as if all this time she'd been waiting by the phone.

"Listen," I said, "I want to apologize for last night. The fact is, I'm trying to hide here, that's why I wasn't very … open to new acquaintances."

Silence. After waiting for about a minute, I said, sighing:

"OK, I get it. Good night."

I was ready to hang up when I heard Kotomi on the other end begging me—again—not to. I felt I had to show some interest in her, though, truth be told, I had no interest whatsoever:

"So, how come you've been here for all this time?"

There was a brief silence followed by a proposal I didn't expect, and which made me immediately regret my overture.

"It's a little hard to talk about it over the phone. Would you like to come over?"

I declined with a (probably) harsh tone, and she apologized right away. She must have sensed my stubborn resistance, because she excused herself over and over with that sweet, high-pitched voice that reminded me of a curly-white, malleable sheep. If she dared to propose such an encounter it was only because, she explained, it was hard enough for her to tell the story behind her retreat under normal circumstances; so it would be even more difficult to do it over the phone.

"I see," I said, blankly.

"So, you *do* understand!"

The funny thing is, I didn't understand anything of her story, which got lost somewhere between her generous interjections and her many expository remarks. Only later did it become clear that she was here because of a man, though I couldn't tell whether she was hiding from him or, on the contrary, waiting for him to come rescue her. A few times she used a word I couldn't make sense of, "haboken," and only two nights later, after two more conversations, did it dawn on me that she meant "heartbroken." She kept saying that she was heartbroken, that life had lost all savor for her, and she had decided to put an end to it. She would have done it already, but couldn't make up her mind about the means—throwing herself from the balcony of the hotel's sixth floor seemed the easiest way, but what if she survived? That's what she was afraid of: survival in some horrible form, which would take away from her the freedom of being in control of her life's end.

"I am telling you all this," she added, "because I've seen you look over the balcony railing. I've seen the look in your eyes, and I know what you were thinking at that moment."

This was more than I was willing to take. Not only was this sheep keeping me awake late at night; she presumed to "know" that I had contemplated suicide, which was the farthest thing from my mind. In my worst moments of depression my greatest fear was that I was going to die, that I was days, or maybe hours away from destiny's slap—a slap that would happen in the most unexpected and unpredictable way, though the paradox was that I was waiting for its arrival all the time. I lived with death breathing behind my back, and I was terrified that I could turn my head and suddenly see it staring me in the face. Kotomi's presumption infuriated me to such a degree that I began to yell at her:

"If you are such an idiot as to want to kill yourself over some *haboken* story, please don't extend your idiocy to others. If I ever decide to kill myself, I would rather do it over my little finger, and certainly not by throwing myself from the balcony. There are more civilized ways of getting it over with, without having to disgust others with your bloody remains scattered all over the asphalt."

In retrospect, I think she must have understood less than half of my speech, because I was speaking fast, angrily swallowing vowels and consonants. After I finished, she apologized—again!—and I could sense the tears welling up in her tensed throat.

"Can you do anything else besides apologizing constantly?"

And I hung up. It still seems strange that this woman I hadn't even seen could put me in such a state, considering that I am usually very calm, so calm, in fact, that the Architect used to get angry because I was (in his words) *made of stone*. To think of it, he did have a point, but he got it backward: it's not that I'm made of stone; it's that I'd like to become stone. And when I travel, it's this radiant quality of the stone exuded by monasteries and old buildings that fascinates me, the stone's eternal tranquility that stems from utter indifference to human struggle and petty passion, an indifference sporting the face of death, but which, in fact, is simply the longing for the divine that all natural elements (stone, water, fire, air) embody. So, in the end, it was probably that part of Kotomi's nature that was so unlike nature itself that annoyed me so. I could sense the agitated movements of that little soul of hers, like machinery that won't stop ticking, full of desire for this and that—now for a man, but a year from now, who knows?—and its meandering reminded me of what I was like years ago, when I was her age, and what I never wanted to be again.

The following day I took a very brave decision: I went out. It had been almost a week since I'd last ventured into the world—an adventure with such a pitiful ending. The reason why I went out is that I'd gotten sick of room service and wanted something else to eat. There was a small grocery store on the street corner, and I was salivating just contemplating the possibility of tasting something new. After a week in the curtained darkness of my room, the sun seemed shinier than ever. I kept blinking, and noticed with surprise that it felt good to have the sun linger over my body. I'd thought I was done with the "joy of living," and was getting ready for (to quote No. 1) the "joy of dying," but life is very stubborn. It clings to us even when we think it has left us.

That's what I was thinking when I returned to the hotel with a bag of groceries, and experienced an unusual tension and negative excitement in the lobby. The faces of the two female receptionists were warped with worry, and hushed whispers came from their taut mouths. A third person, a man, was on the phone, explaining something in an urgent tone. I asked the receptionists what was the matter, but they just stared at me with blank faces. As I was about to call the elevator, a guest whispered, "There was an accident … A woman fell …" There was something in the way he said it that made my heart skip a beat. I took the elevator and, as I stepped out of it on the sixth floor, a foreboding took hold of me. I couldn't articulate what I was afraid of, but I knew, or rather, my stomach knew that something horrible had happened. I opened the door, dropped my groceries on the floor, and went straight to the balcony. And I knew the truth before my eyes could regain their focus and see the body flattened on the ground like a drawing, with the white dress fluttering in the wind—an abandoned flag clinging to a soulless pole.

* * *

Another week has passed since Kotomi's body lay on the ground with such pathetic desolation—pathetic because even its desolation was on a small scale, birdlike, or even sheeplike, deprived of the grandeur of tragedy. Yes, it's been another week since I've stepped out of my room. It's not that I feel particularly guilty—why should I? She was determined to do it, and she would have done it anyhow; besides, there is nothing I dislike more than the discourse, which, under the pretext of honoring "life" at any price, ends up dishonoring individual will and choice. If someone wants to commit suicide, let them do it. It's probably better for everybody. No, it's not the guilt that bothered me. It's the thought that this sheeplike woman had the courage to do something I was incapable of. I pictured her by the balcony railing in her white summer dress, grasping it and staring into the void, then climbing it and, with her legs dangling in the air, sitting there—for how long? A second? A minute? Half an hour?—attempting the hardest thing of all: to cut the thread between being and nonbeing, to accept in her mind and in her body that a few seconds later she would be no more. The courage of the instant when she jumped, when she let go of that steel rail, when she knew ... *That* instant when Kotomi was simultaneously closer to a superhuman being *and* a thing, when she was turned into a nonhuman, was something I could only aspire to.

I therefore began to think of Kotomi with unhoped-for reverence, reverence for what is beyond our powers, and alluring for that very reason. I understood only too well the mistake one makes in such a situation by taking an accident—even if the accident was provoked by one's will—and elevating it to the seducing power of myth. Pretty soon the sheep-woman of such a story is turned into a heroine, and the sheep-worshippers are hanging a new icon on their walls. And so I wavered between reverence and lucidity by telling myself with renewed conviction, "See … if *she* could do it, then …" I never finished the thought: *then* what? But I kept repeating these words like an axiom, or a zinger, or a nursery rhyme, hoping they would push me toward the vanishing point where everything would be illuminated by a revelation that couldn't but appear at the right moment. So it was that I groped in darkness in the curtained room, hanging onto the morsels I'd bought at the street corner, and which would soon be gone, cautiously savoring the puffy, custard-filled pastries and the various dry snacks in their vacuum-sealed containers, as I let myself slide down the fairytale rays of light of Korean soap operas, munching and sliding lower and lower with a lightness of being that made it hard to distinguish between my opaque body and the deceptively clear light. I remembered how, when I was little, I used to think that the actors lived inside the TV, and kept searching for them at its back only to run into frustrating wires, rectangular metal boxes, and black plastic. Somehow that ugly machine could hold inside of it all those beautiful actors that made it come to life every morning when we turned it on. At night, the actors went to sleep, and so did the machine that hosted them.

Opening another box of sweets—these were filled with some kind of chestnut cream—I thought I wouldn't mind living inside the TV. Stuffing my mouth with a large piece of chestnut-filled pastry, I saw myself entering the screened black box and joining the tortuous dramas of daughters separated at birth from their mothers, in love with their sisters' husbands, or dying a premature death only to come back to life a few episodes later, and as I entered the box, my white dress—Kotomi's dress!—got caught in one of the machine's intestines, and there I was: inside the box with all those colorful people around me, while a tiny part of the dress remained flapping in the black-and-white world outside, a remnant of a world I had once belonged to and which was now lost to me because (and I thought of this with broken laughter) I was now the architect of my own disappearance, having entombed myself in this box, which was nothing more or less than my own cathedral.

Santa Cruz, California, 2012–2014

ACKNOWLEDGMENTS

My thanks go to Antonio Viscardi for his advice regarding technical questions about architecture, and to Stephen Kessler and Elizabeth Mckenzie for being the first readers of this novel. I am also grateful to the Millay Colony and the Ragdale Foundation for providing me with the space and peace necessary to work on this book. An excerpt from this novel appeared in *Phren-Z*. No. 6, Spring 2013, as "A Summer with Aunt Susanna."

ALSO FROM
NEW EUROPE BOOKS

978-1-7345379-3-2

A scintillating, comic novel about one young American and his fellow expats caught up in a student loan scheme in an imaginary Eastern European capital

"*Visegrad* is very funny and very insightful—into Central Europe, into the US, into the expat mind."

—**Arthur Phillips, author of *Prague* and *The King at the Edge of the World***

ALSO FROM
NEW EUROPE BOOKS

978-0-9973169-2-6

Praise for the first edition:

"A commendable feat. . . . Jankowski writes in an intelligent, accessible style"   *—Library Journal*

"Accessible and stimulating. . . . A good resource for teachers, students, and all those with roots in this part of the world."   *—CHOICE*

"Recommended reading for anyone heading to the former Eastern Bloc."   *—Traveller,* **easyJet's inflight magazine**

ALSO FROM
NEW EUROPE BOOKS

978-1-7345379-1-8

A journalist's personal account of why one small European nation's path away from liberal democracy carries vital lessons for us all

"Skytt's great service to the reader is that he shows why so many Hungarians love Viktor Orbán so much. And through that gateway, he strides out onto the bigger political battlefield, to help us understand: why do so many people round the world love other leaders like Viktor Orban so much?"
—from the foreword by Nick Thorpe, BBC Central Europe Correspondent

Also Available
from New Europe Books

ABOUT THE AUTHOR

Alta Ifland is the author of *The Wife Who Wasn't* (New Europe Books, 2021), of which the *Los Angeles Review of Books* wrote, "This comedy of errors is a page-turner, where a mail-order bride service, enough love triangles to boggle the mind, a stolen Egon Schiele painting, and a devastating fire lead the worlds of Santa Barbara and Chișinău to collide." She was born in Romania, took part in the overthrow of its communist dictatorship, and emigrated to the United States in 1991. After earning a PhD in French language and literature, and several years of university teaching, Ifland now works as a fulltime writer, book reviewer, and translator (from/into French and Romanian). She is also the author of two books of short stories—*Elegy for a Fabulous World* (2010 finalist for the Northern California Book Award in Fiction) and *Death-in-a-Box* (2010 Subito Press Fiction Prize)— and two collections of prose poems, including *Voix de Glace/ Voice of Ice* (bilingual, self-translated, 2008 Louis Guillaume Prize). After many years in California, she lives currently in France.